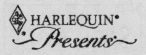

HARLEQUIN®
Presents

Welcome to the September 2008 collection of
Harlequin Presents!

This month, be sure to read favorite author
Penny Jordan's *Virgin for the Billionaire's Taking*,
in which virginal Keira is whisked off to the exotic
world of handsome Jay! Michelle Reid brings you a
fabulous tale of a ruthless Italian's convenient bride
in *The De Santis Marriage,* while Carol Marinelli's
gorgeous tycoon wants revenge on innocent Caitlyn
in *Italian Boss, Ruthless Revenge.* And don't miss
the final story in Carole Mortimer's brilliant trilogy
THE SICILIANS, *The Sicilian's Innocent Mistress!*
Abby Green brings you the society wedding of
the year in *The Kouros Marriage Revenge,* and in
Chantelle Shaw's *At The Sheikh's Bidding,* Erin's life
is changed forever when she discovers her adopted
son is heir to a desert kingdom!

Also this month, new author Heidi Rice delivers a
sizzling, sexy boss in *The Tycoon's Very Personal
Assistant,* and in Ally Blake's *The Magnate's Indecent
Proposal,* an ordinary girl is faced with a millionaire
who's way out of her league. Enjoy!

We'd love to hear what you think about Harlequin
Presents. E-mail us at Presents@hmb.co.uk or join
in the discussions at www.iheartpresents.com and
www.sensationalromance.blogspot.com, where
you'll also find more information about books and
authors!

THE SICILIANS

They seek passion—at any price!

A new series by Carole Mortimer

Sicilian heroes—with revenge in mind and romance in their destinies!

The Sicilian's Ruthless Marriage Revenge
July 2008

At the Sicilian Count's Command
August 2008

The Sicilian's Innocent Mistress
September 2008

Carole Mortimer

THE SICILIAN'S INNOCENT MISTRESS

THE
SICILIANS

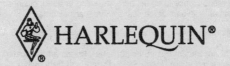

HARLEQUIN®

TORONTO • NEW YORK • LONDON
AMSTERDAM • PARIS • SYDNEY • HAMBURG
STOCKHOLM • ATHENS • TOKYO • MILAN • MADRID
PRAGUE • WARSAW • BUDAPEST • AUCKLAND

ISBN-13: 978-0-373-12758-0
ISBN-10:   0-373-12758-8

THE SICILIAN'S INNOCENT MISTRESS

First North American Publication 2008.

www.eHarlequin.com

Printed in U.S.A.

All about the author...
Carole Mortimer

CAROLE MORTIMER is one of Harlequin's most popular and prolific authors. Since her first novel was published in 1979, this British writer has shown no sign of slowing her pace. In fact, she has published more than 125 books to date!

Carole was born in a village in England that she claims was so small "if you blinked as you drove through it you could miss seeing it completely!" She adds that her parents still live in the house where she was born, and her two brothers live very close by.

Carole's early ambition to become a nurse came to an abrupt end after only one year of training, due to a weakness in her back, suffered after a fall. Instead she went on to work in the computer department of a well-known stationery company.

During her time there, Carole made her first attempt at writing a novel for Harlequin. "The manuscript was far too short and the plotline not up to standard, so I naturally received a rejection slip," she says. "Not taking rejection well, I went off in a sulk for two years before deciding to have another go." Her second manuscript was accepted, beginning a long and fruitful career. She says she has "enjoyed every moment of it!"

Carole lives "in a most beautiful part of Britain" with her husband and children.

"I really do enjoy my writing, and have every intention of continuing to do so for another twenty years!"

CHAPTER ONE

'SO, WHICH look do you think is going to attract the attention of a heartbreaker like film producer Luc Gambrelli?' Darci prompted Kerry consideringly, as she threw open the door to her wardrobe and brought out a white dress. 'The demure virgin?'

She held the garment against her, its plain styling covering her tall slenderness from neck to knee. She pulled her heavy length of red hair away from the delicate lines of her heart-shaped face, at the same time lowering her head, her expression youthfully coy as she looked at Kerry with moss-green eyes through long dark lashes.

Her flatmate and long-term friend laughed softly as she sat on the bed, watching the display. 'Or…?' Kerry queried smilingly.

'Or sexy vamp?' Darci threw the white dress down on the bed and pulled out a slinky black gown, its ribbon shoulder straps, low neckline, body-hugging style and length—three inches above the knee—leaving very little to the imagination as she held it against her, releasing her hair to fluff its long, fiery length enticingly about her face and shoulders as she adopted a deliberately seductive pose.

'Hmm.' Kerry grimaced. 'Somewhere in between the two,

I think. Grant once told me that every man's perfect fantasy woman is one who's as beautiful and charming as an angel in public and as sexy as a she-devil in his bed!'

Darci's brows rose. 'My big brother told you that?'

'Years ago, at university.' Kerry, a tiny brunette, laughed at Darci's surprised expression. 'I think we had all just come home from a party at the time, and he was bemoaning the fact that he doubted he was ever going to meet his perfect woman.'

'Well, he was right about that, anyway; at twenty-eight he's still a bachelor. In fact, just like me, there isn't a permanent relationship in sight,' Darci added with a slight frown. 'If there was, he wouldn't have asked me to accompany him to his latest film premiere!'

Exactly five minutes older than Darci, her twin brother was an extremely successful film director. He had scaled the heady heights to superstardom during the last four years, his last two films having been box office hits. Grant was hoping to add to his current run of success with the premiere of his latest film the following evening. A premiere where, as the producer of the film, Luc Gambrelli was also going to be in attendance.

A delicious coincidence too convenient to resist as far as Darci was concerned...

She looked at the two dresses critically. 'So, somewhere in between, you think...? Of course it would probably help if I knew whether Luc Gambrelli preferred redheads to brunettes or blondes.'

'Depends on the day of the week, I expect,' Kerry dismissed sagely. 'Monday a blonde. Tuesday a brunette. Wednesday a redhead. Et cetera. From the gossip about him in the newspapers over the years, he appears to have a different woman for each day of the week,' she explained, at Darci's puzzled look.

Darci pondered her friend's words. 'Then we can only hope that it's redheads on a Thursday evening!'

Her friend gave her a rueful smile. 'You really intend going through with this…?'

'And hopefully giving Luc Gambrelli a taste of his own heartless medicine?' Darci said distractedly, as she began another search through her wardrobe for the perfect dress to wear tomorrow evening. 'He broke Mellie's heart, remember. Of course I'm going to get Grant to introduce the two of us at the premiere in the hope of attracting his attention—and then I shall have the pleasure of giving him one almighty set-down if he does show any interest. It's about time some woman let the arrogant Luc Gambrelli know that every female he meets isn't going to swoon at his feet!' she added with determination.

'Isn't being rude to someone as powerful as film producer Luc Gambrelli possibly going to have fall-out and damage Grant's career?' Kerry responded.

'That's the best part.' Darci grinned. 'My big brother is so much the golden boy movie director at the moment that he simply can't be touched!'

Kerry still looked worried. 'Yet from what I've read, the film world is a precarious one; someone can be the darling of the moment one minute and a total outcast the next!'

'Do you really think Luc Gambrelli would be petty enough to take his disappointment out on Grant?' Darci said disbelievingly.

'He might,' Kerry returned.

Darci laughed as she bent down to hug the other woman. 'You always were the worrier amongst us!' she told Kerry affectionately, knowing that if it weren't for her friend's caution in earlier years she would have got into many more scrapes than she had, her own nature—part of being a redhead, perhaps?—having been much more impetuous.

And Darci had no intention of backing off from Luc Gambrelli. Not after what he had done to Mellie…

'You do realise that Luc Gambrelli will probably be with someone tomorrow evening…?' Kerry persisted.

'That's where you're wrong,' Darci announced with satisfaction. 'Grant told me that Luc Gambrelli is escorting the female lead, Jackie Tunbridge. She's new to all this, and a little nervous, and apparently Luc Gambrelli has been a little more circumspect in who he takes where recently.' She paused to consider for a moment, then continued, 'Grant says it's because he doesn't want to get caught in the marital trap, like his brother and his cousin. Count Wolf Gambrelli and Cesare Gambrelli,' she explained, as Kerry looked totally blank.

'Luc Gambrelli is related to those two?' Kerry gasped after a few seconds.

Darci nodded. 'His brother is the Count, no less,' she confirmed, still searching through her wardrobe for exactly the right dress to wear tomorrow evening. 'It's no good,' she conceded, as she turned back into the bedroom decisively. 'I'll have to go out tomorrow and look for something new.'

'But you hate shopping for new clothes,' her friend reminded her.

Darci scowled. 'For the chance to put the oh-I-think-I'm-so-wonderful Luc Gambrelli firmly in his place I'll make an exception! Kerry, I know you don't think this is a good idea,' she said, as Kerry carried on looking doubtful. 'But the man really can't be allowed to just cold-heartedly break the heart of one of my very best friends without some sort of retaliation!'

Kerry, Mellie and Darci had been at school together, and then had stuck with each other while taking further education courses in London: Kerry had taken a degree in History, Mellie had gone to drama school and Darci had chosen Medicine. Grant, having known Darci's old friends well, and having attended university, too, had joined them in sharing a house during those years of studying.

The passing years had forged a bond between the four of them that was as close, if not closer, than family; if one of them was hurt, the others felt it, too.

And then, six weeks ago, Mellie's tender heart had been broken by the heartless Luc Gambrelli!

After university Grant had gone to Los Angeles, and the three women had taken another apartment together in London. Then, six months ago, Mellie—after some mild success on the London stage—had gone to Los Angeles, too, in order to look for acting roles.

Which was how she had met and fallen in love with the famous film producer Luc Gambrelli.

The two had got together at a party—Luc Gambrelli apparently dazzling Mellie completely when he'd assured her that she was perfect for a part in the film he was shortly going to put into production.

Kerry and Darci had followed the Italian film producer's seduction of Mellie via their friend's frequent telephone calls and e-mails, and she'd waxed lyrical about how wonderful he was, how he had swept her off her feet, pursuing her relentlessly as he showered her with flowers and gifts until his conquest was secure and Mellie was head-over-heels in love with him and more than eager to share his bed. An experience Mellie had related to her two friends in erotic detail.

After which the heartless pig had just disappeared out of Mellie's life, as had the prospective part in his film, leaving her broken-hearted as she realised she had fallen for the oldest trick in the book when it came to acting—the casting couch. Or, in this case, Luc Gambrelli's silk-sheeted bed!

If all Darci managed to do tomorrow evening was get Grant to introduce her to Luc Gambrelli, and then she succeeded in giving the man the knock to his super-ego that he so richly deserved, she would be happy.

All without telling him that she was a friend of Mellie's, of course; it would be just too humiliating for Mellie if Luc Gambrelli were to realise she had really fallen for him in a big way.

Of course an even better set-down would have been if Mellie herself had accompanied Grant to the premiere. But that would have involved telling Grant of Mellie's humiliation, and for Mellie's sake, Darci was trying to avoid doing that.

'I think you're mad to go within twenty feet of all that lethal charm, darling,' Kerry told her admiringly. 'And of course, there's always the possibility that it may just backfire on you,' she added.

'You mean, he really may not like redheads?' Darci replied.

'This redhead?' Kerry looked at Darci consideringly before responding loyally, 'Not a chance! You're incredibly beautiful and very sexy. As proven by the amount of hearts you've left broken along the wayside in the last few years!'

If Darci had, then it hadn't been deliberate. She had just been pretty single-minded about her career—to the point where relationships hadn't featured too strongly in her life, and certainly none of a permanent nature. There simply hadn't been the time for that, as well as her work.

'So what did you mean about it backfiring...?' she said slowly.

Kerry sighed. 'Has it ever occurred to you that once you've actually met the man, you might just find Luc Gambrelli as devastatingly irresistible as every other female on the planet has? That instead of taking delight in coldly shunning him you might just end up falling for all that Mediterranean charm yourself?' she warned wryly.

'No chance,' Darci assured her with certainty. 'Sicilian playboys with more money than morals hold absolutely no appeal for me!'

'Have you seen this Sicilian playboy?' Kerry teased.

Well, of course Darci had seen photographs of Luc Gambrelli; the man appeared in the gossip columns of newspapers and magazines all the time as he escorted one beautiful actress or another.

He was more than six feet tall, with overlong hair the colour of burnished gold, and his tanned face was all hard, sculptured angles that were enough to make a woman's pulse race just to look at him. Luc Gambrelli wasn't only one of the most elusive bachelors in the world, he was also one of the most arrogantly attractive.

Nevertheless, Luc Gambrelli, the multimillionaire Sicilian who changed his women as often as he changed the black silk sheets on his bed, was about to meet the one woman who had no intention of falling for his devastating charm or succumbing to his irresistible seduction.

He was about to meet the totally impervious and vengeful Darci....

CHAPTER TWO

'DID you see much of Mellie while you were in Los Angeles?' Darci prompted her brother lightly.

'Mellie?' Grant repeated, as he turned from surveying the crowded reception room at the glittering post-premiere party.

Darci gave him a coy smile, 'Yes, you know—Mellie. Old schoolfriend of mine. We all shared a flat together a few years ago.'

'Very funny,' her brother drawled. 'I just wondered at your interest, that's all.'

Darci's interest was in knowing whether or not Grant knew of Mellie's ill-fated involvement with Luc Gambrelli!

'Perhaps the exulted film director Grant Wilde is far too superior now to remember his old friends…?' she continued to tease her brother.

'Very funny!' Grant came back. 'And, yes, I did see Mellie a couple of times,' he confirmed. 'But I— Oh—hi there.' He turned to greet someone smilingly.

'Would you care to introduce me to your beautiful partner for the evening, Grant…?' Luc Gambrelli asked huskily, strolling over to join the young movie director and the entrancingly lovely woman who stood at his side, drinking a glass of the champagne that was flowing freely now that the after-party was in full swing.

The premiere had been a success as far as the critics invited to the party were concerned, although the newspapers tomorrow morning would probably be more revealing.

Luc had been aware of the striking redhead at Grant Wilde's side earlier this evening the moment she entered the theatre on the other man's arm. She was far too beautiful to be overlooked, even amongst this glittering crowd of celebrities. Her long red hair was like that of a woman in a pre-Raphaelite painting, her eyes a clear lucent green, her complexion creamy smooth, with a tiny smattering of freckles across the bridge of her nose, her lips a full sensual pout—and as for that body, shown to advantage in a clinging green gown!

She was very slender, with long shapely legs, narrow hips and a flat abdomen, but in contrast her breasts—bare beneath that clinging gown, Luc felt certain!—were full and pert, their creamy swell tantalisingly visible above the low neckline of her gown.

His curiosity had been piqued earlier, as her coolly dismissive gaze had swept over the crowded foyer. Those eyes the colour of moss—an exact match to the gown she wore, which clung so enticingly to that curvaceous body—had paused on him momentarily, before she had turned away, uninterested.

Enough to quicken the interest of any red-blooded man!

And especially one who had already found her so immediately attractive...

There hadn't been time for any introductions before the film showing, but Luc had been determined to meet her once they moved on to the party afterwards.

She was even more beautiful close to: her skin satiny

smooth, those green eyes mesmerising through lowered dark lashes, a deep peach gloss on the pout of her lips, her hair the most incredible shade of red as it tumbled over her bare shoulders almost down to her waist. And, being several inches taller than her, even in her high-heeled sandals, Luc had more than a glimpse of that amazing cleavage!

His gaze was heated as he looked at her from beneath hooded lids, his tongue moving across his lips as he imagined what it would be like to view that cleavage, that amazing body, without the benefit of the green gown, to kiss her, taste her, touch her…

Having been pursued—and having allowed himself to be captured for a short time—by some of the most beautiful women in the world, Luc found his instantaneous response to this woman's beauty something of a novelty.

Although, as he knew from his jaded experience, the novelty wouldn't last any longer than it took to entice her into his bed!

If he could entice her into his bed.

The cool lack of interest that he had seen in her eyes earlier, as her gaze had swept over him so dismissively, hadn't abated in the slightest as she looked up at him now, from beneath those long, dark lashes.

'Of course, Luc,' Grant answered him warmly. 'This is my twin sister, Darci Wilde. Darci—Luc Gambrelli,' he introduced them.

Grant's *sister*?

This woman was Grant's twin sister?

The two couldn't have been more unalike; Grant was a six foot blond, and the woman at his side a tall red-haired siren. The only features they appeared to have in common were their height and those moss-green eyes.

'Darci,' Luc acknowledged, his dark gaze holding hers as, instead of shaking the hand she held out to him, he raised it to brush his lips across her creamy knuckles.

Her hand felt soft and warm in his, her fingers long and slender, and her perfume—something elusively musky—at once assailed his senses.

Darci guardedly returned Luc Gambrelli's gaze from beneath lowered lashes, even as she congratulated herself on the fact that she hadn't had to ask to be introduced to him after all—that he had come to her.

Not that she was too surprised at that. She had noted his dark gaze on her when she'd arrived with Grant earlier this evening, and several more times when she'd happened to surreptitiously glance his way. No doubt in a theatre full of celebrities the fact that he had no idea who she was had something to do with that interest.

Although she was a little less pleased with her success now, as he bent his head over her hand, those dark eyes openly flirting with hers as his lips brushed against her skin.

Kerry's warning came back to haunt her...

Aged in his midthirties, Luc Gambrelli was just as lethally attractive as he looked in media photos. But more so. The flesh-and-blood man exuded a leashed power, the force of which couldn't possibly be captured in a photograph. His body was lithe and muscled, in a black dinner suit, snowy-white shirt and black tie, and that overlong burnished gold hair was completely at odds with his olive complexion, his deep chocolate-brown eyes and very white teeth. He raised his head to give Darci a slow, wolfishly appreciative smile while still maintaining his hold on her hand.

But his reputation, and the cold-hearted way he had used

and then discarded Mellie, breaking her heart in the process, made Darci determined not to be in the least impressed by his heart-stopping good looks, that pulse-racing Sicilian charm, or the nerve-tingling huskiness of his voice as it moved as silkily across her flesh as his lips had seconds earlier.

'Mr Gambrelli,' she returned coolly, as she extricated her hand from his, and she returned his gaze defiantly but uninterestedly.

'Please call me Luc,' he invited, heavy lids narrowed now over speculative brown eyes.

'Of course.' She gave a terse nod, deliberately not returning the politeness.

'And are you involved in movie-making, too, Darci?' he enquired. 'An actress, perhaps—?'

'I'm afraid not.' Darci's reply was dismissive as she levelly returned his flirtatious gaze.

A look that more than piqued Luc's interest. 'I believe Jackie is in need of your assistance in handling the media, Grant,' he told the younger man lazily, while keeping his gaze firmly fixed on the beautiful Darci.

'Hell,' Grant muttered, as he turned and saw that Jackie, a complete newcomer to the stardom that had hit her overnight after starring in his movie, was stuck in a corner with a few of the more voracious members of the press. 'I had better go and rescue her,' he said. 'Darci—'

'I will ensure that Darci does not become too bored in your absence,' Luc assured the other man, and he reached out to once again take hold of Darci's hand and draw it into the crook of his arm.

This man didn't miss a trick, did he? Darci acknowledged with an inward scowl, as she felt the hard, disturbing warmth of Luc Gambrelli's body against her arm as he anchored her to his side.

Grant grinned at the older man. 'Take it easy on my little sister, hmm, Luc…?' he warned dryly.

Luc gave the other man a mocking inclination of his head, totally aware of the tension in Darci Wilde's body as she stood beside him.

Totally aware of everything about her. From the glorious scented red hair that he longed to bury his face in, to the beauty of her red-lacquered toes that he wanted to kiss through the black strappy evening sandals she wore. Before slowly working his way up the sultry curves of the rest of her body to those voluptuous breasts….

Most men, he knew, had a particular part of a woman's body that they preferred to any other—legs, bottom or breasts. But Luc couldn't say he had ever before thought of a woman's breasts as being his own particular preference. He would definitely make Darci Wilde the exception!

Grant's grin widened. 'I should warn you, Luc—it takes a lot to impress my little sister,' he advised, before strolling off determinedly to rescue his leading lady.

Darci gave a rueful smile as her brother left her alone with this wolf—in wolf's clothing!—without so much as a backward glance.

Not that Grant had any idea of her ambivalent feelings towards the Sicilian film producer. There were some things you didn't confide even in a twin, and Mellie's humiliation at Luc Gambrelli's hands was definitely one of them!

But, even so, her brother had to be well aware of Luc Gambrelli's reputation with women—

On second thoughts, Grant probably saw leaving her to the legendary lethal charms of Luc Gambrelli as a huge joke!

Although whether Grant intended that joke to be on her or on Luc Gambrelli, she wasn't quite sure. Grant was as aware of her own elusiveness when it came to relationships as he had to be of the other man's will-o'-the-wisp attitude towards them.

She turned to the man standing so arrogantly beside her. 'I believe you did that on purpose,' she murmured mockingly.

'True,' Luc Gambrelli drawled unrepentantly. 'Is what Grant said also true, Darci?' he prompted as he moved slightly, effectively cutting her off from the rest of the room.

'That I'm not easily impressed?' she rejoined. 'What do you think?' she prompted provocatively.

He raised dark blond brows over those melting chocolate-brown eyes. 'I don't believe you are ready yet to hear what I'm thinking,' he came back throatily.

Darci blinked as he returned her provocation tenfold, the intimacy of his tone telling her exactly along what line his thoughts were wandering.

As if the dark caress of his stare as he slowly moved it across her face to trail down the length of her body wasn't already making her completely aware of that!

Well, she wasn't some shrinking violet, or a relatively unknown actress who was hoping he would give her a break in her career; she was twenty-eight years old and a doctor, and she was going to take great delight in letting this man know that she really wasn't impressed by anything about him.

She stepped back, deliberately removing her hand from Luc Gambrelli's arm as she did so, amazed at how much easier she found it to breathe now that she was no longer so aware of the hard warmth of his body. 'Try me,' she invited challengingly.

Appreciation lit those dark eyes as he grinned at her. 'Would you like a detailed account or just an overview?' he came back easily, so obviously a consummate flirt.

Darci calmly took a sip of her champagne as she seemed to give the question some thought, inwardly fighting a battle not to wipe the confident smile off Luc Gambrelli's arrogant face. Not yet, anyway.

She'd had every intention of having the pleasure of giving Luc Gambrelli a royal set-down this evening, *if* he should show interest in her, to let him know that he really couldn't have every woman he wanted. But just these few minutes in his company had shown her that his interest in her was certain. Those dark brown eyes easily conveyed the depth of his physical attraction to her.

So much so that Darci couldn't help wondering if she shouldn't take this a step further than just this evening....

There were a couple of ifs involved in that plan, of course....

If Luc Gambrelli should actually ask to see her again.

If she had the nerve to actually agree to seeing him again, knowing she had no intention of keeping that date!

She looked up at Luc and allowed her green eyes to meet his unblinkingly. 'The detailed account, I think,' she invited coquettishly.

Grant Wilde's sister was becoming more and more of a surprise to him the longer he spent in her company, Luc acknowledged appreciatively; he was no longer just attracted to her luscious body, but also to the sharp edge of her tongue and the intelligence he could read in the depths of those moss-green eyes.

She was Grant's twin, so Luc knew she had to be aged in her late twenties, and, beautiful as she was, she must have received more than her fair share of male attention. And it was attention she obviously had no difficulty in dealing with.

The fact that there wasn't even the slightest blush on her cheeks as she encouraged him to voice the intimacies he would like to share with her confirmed that.

He gave a slight inclination of his head. 'Perhaps we should go somewhere a little more—private, for this conversation?' he suggested softly.

Darci continued to survey him coolly. 'I was only suggesting that you tell me your thoughts, Mr Gambrelli—not that we put any of them into action!' she told him tartly.

'Ah.' He smiled. 'My mistake.'

'Indeed,' she snapped waspishly, those green eyes glittering warningly.

Luc allowed his gaze to once again move appreciatively over the beauty of her face. Darci Wilde, he decided, was something of a contradiction; that glorious abundance of red hair, the lush curve of her breasts and the slenderness of her waist and thighs were so totally feminine, and yet at the same time were in total contrast to that sharp flick of her tongue.

It was a contrast he was finding more and more intriguing by the minute!

Perhaps not such a good idea…

Only a year ago there had been three Gambrelli bachelors: his cousin, Cesare, his brother, Wolf, and Luc himself. But a year ago Cesare had fallen in love with Robin, and then, four months later, the two of them had married. Only three months ago Wolf had married his beloved Angel. Leaving Luc as the only one who remained single.

A status quo that he was absolutely determined to keep!

So much so that he had avoided entering any relationships at all since his brother Wolf's wedding.

But telling Darci Wilde of the ways in which he would like to make love to her wasn't a relationship, was it?

'Very well. As you insist.' His voice lowered huskily. 'First of all I would like to kiss you. Just your mouth, you understand? It's such a—delicious mouth,' he added, as his heated gaze locked onto her peach pout. 'Soft. And full. And so tempting. Yes, I would very much like to kiss you,' he confirmed. 'To taste you. To let my tongue explore you.'

Darci could feel the heat creeping into her body as the intimacy in Luc Gambrelli's voice moved across and into her. She was aware of the way her breasts had swelled, their nipples hard and tingling, of the heat moving between her thighs.

Not exactly what she had planned to happen when she'd decided to call this man's bluff!

'And while I am kissing you,' Luc Gambrelli continued in that low, sensuous voice, 'I would like to thread my fingers into your beautiful hair, to feel its silky softness, to tangle it about my fingers as we deepen the kiss. And then I would like to release one of my hands to run the zip of your dress slowly down your spine, touching you as I do so, caressing the smoothness of your bare skin as I allow the gown to drop to the floor. Underneath the gown you would be wearing nothing but a pair of silk panties—black, I think,' he added, as he looked over her with slow consideration, 'and sheer flesh-coloured stockings—'

'Are you trying to shock me, Mr Gambrelli?' Darci cut in quickly, hopefully hiding her inner discomfort at the fact that he had guessed exactly what she was—or rather, wasn't!—wearing beneath her gown.

No doubt, experienced lover that he was, Luc Gambrelli was more than capable of undressing a woman with just his eyes, she acknowledged hardly.

'Am I succeeding?' he enquired, those dark eyes glinting with a devilish humour.

Something else Darci hadn't been prepared for…

She had expected Luc Gambrelli to be as good-looking as sin. And he was.

She had expected him to be arrogant. And he was most definitely that.

But what she hadn't expected was that he would also have a wicked—and very appealing—sense of humour!

'Not in the least,' she assured him with calm dismissal, as she took another sip of her champagne.

'Good—because I haven't got to the best part yet,' he murmured assuredly, laughter glinting in those dark eyes. 'Once I had you out of your dress I would kneel at your feet, paying homage to your beautiful breasts with my lips and tongue on the way down, and then I would slowly slide off your silk panties—'

'I'm sure it's fascinating to hear your fantasies, Mr Gambrelli.' Her scathing tone told him she considered it the opposite. 'But then they are just fantasies, aren't they?'

'For the moment,' he agreed, and once again his gaze fixed caressingly on the full pout of her mouth.

Darci knew exactly the effect her looks had on men of all ages—how her height, her unruly red hair and voluptuous breasts prevented most men from taking her seriously. She had been fighting against that prejudice all her life, but especially during her years of training to be a doctor. In fact, she was still fighting it with the male staff at the hospital where she worked. And with some of the patients, too—young men considering her easy bait for their teasing, and most older men reluctant to let an attractive young female doctor care for them at all.

The fact that Luc Gambrelli had taken one look at her and decided not to take her seriously, either, only made her see red!

She was more determined than ever that he needed to be taught a salutary lesson—and that was never to underestimate a woman scorned or, in this case, never to underestimate the *friend* of a woman scorned!

'As you said earlier, Luc, this is hardly the place for this sort of conversation,' she dismissed, with a lightness she was far from feeling. Her breasts ached—her nipples actually throbbed!—and there was a dampness between her thighs from just listening to this man talk about making love to her.

'Where would you consider the right place to be?' he encouraged naughtily.

Nowhere, as far as this mesmerising man was concerned!

'Fascinating as this conversation has been, Luc, I think it's probably time I rejoined Grant,' she replied smartly. 'I— What do you think you're doing?' She frowned as Luc Gambrelli reached out and grasped her bare arm, his long fingers dark against her much paler skin.

Yes, what *was* he doing? Luc wondered impatiently.

Darci Wilde was beautiful, yes. Desirable. Intelligent, too. Certainly quick-witted enough to hold his interest. But wasn't this an interest, raw as he still was from Wolf and Cesare's defection to the married state, that Luc was trying to avoid at all costs?

But Darci was so incredibly beautiful, and he was already

aroused just from talking about making love to her deliciously sensual body…

'I wonder if you would care to have dinner with me one evening?' he asked smoothly, not at all sure of the wisdom of seeing this woman again, but aware that his caution stood little chance of winning out when his body throbbed with a need to know her better.

An urgent need.

A need that at the moment far outweighed those feelings of caution.

Darci looked up at Luc Gambrelli for several long minutes, torn between the satisfaction of having this man invite her out after all, and the fact that, now she had actually spent some time in Luc Gambrelli's company, she appreciated that Kerry's warning of yesterday had some merit.

Not that there had ever been any real chance of her actually falling for Luc Gambrelli—not after the way he had treated Mellie. But at the same time Darci had to acknowledge that he really was much more lethally attractive in the flesh. His unusual colouring and undeniable good looks were mesmerising, his every movement was one of elegantly leashed power, and that wicked sense of humour was definitely more appealing than it should be.

His description of how he wanted to make love to her hadn't been in the least calming, either!

'Perhaps if I were to assure you, despite what I have just described, that you won't be on the menu…?' He mocked her lengthy silence.

Darci's mouth tightened at the challenge. 'Perhaps I should assure you that you won't be, either!' she came back acidly.

Those dark eyes warmed appreciatively. 'Tomorrow evening, then? Say eight o'clock?'

'I'm busy tomorrow evening,' she took great satisfaction in telling him.

It was the truth, after all; she had a late shift at the hospital tomorrow. But even if she hadn't, she would have made an excuse not to meet him tomorrow evening. If only to show him she was less than eager to see him again.

The fact that the warmth had faded slightly from those dark eyes, his lips thinning, more than justified her refusal.

No doubt he was used to a more enthusiastic response to his invitations.

No doubt most women would have put off any previous engagement in order to have dinner with him tomorrow or any other evening he suggested.

Well, as Luc Gambrelli was going to learn, Darci wasn't most women.

And in his case forewarned had definitely been fore-armed!

She had no doubt, despite her own reluctance when it came to relationships, that she would have been totally bowled over by his deadly charm if she hadn't already known what a heartless bastard he really was.

'Saturday evening?' he pressed abruptly.

Darci deliberately gave the alternative suggestion some thought, knowing as she glanced at his face from beneath lowered lashes that the egotistical Luc Gambrelli wasn't best pleased by her obvious hesitation.

He was going to be less pleased when she didn't even turn up for their dinner date!

'Why not?' she finally accepted offhandedly. 'As long as you intend taking me somewhere sinfully expensive.' She looked up at him beguilingly, wondering how he liked the idea of literally being used as a meal-ticket.

He didn't, if the tightening of his mouth and the narrowing of his gaze was anything to go by!

Although it was an emotion he quickly masked as he gave a shrug of those broad shoulders. 'I'm sure I can find somewhere appropriately sinful,' he replied.

'Sinfully expensive,' Darci corrected—did this man have to reduce everything to the nerve-tinglingly sensual?

'Of course,' he drawled, the confident warmth back in those dark eyes as he easily held her gaze and released his grip on her arm to trail his fingers caressingly downwards.

Darci's breath caught in her throat at the headiness caused by that light touch. Her skin actually seemed to tingle, her own fingers contracting slightly as his thumb intimately stroked the palm of her hand.

It was deliberate seduction, she told herself firmly. Something this man was a master at. In fact, he probably had a diploma on his bedroom wall—as well as several dozen notches on his bedpost!—to testify to his expertise on the subject!

Telling herself that didn't help in the slightest as those long tapered fingers linked with hers and he once again lifted her hand to his lips, his breath warm against her skin as he brushed his mouth against her knuckles, his dark eyes easily holding hers as his tongue rasped briefly—tasting?—where his lips had just kissed.

A master of seduction? The man should come with a public health warning!

No wonder poor Mellie had fallen victim to Luc's advances...

'Until Saturday evening, then, Darci,' he confirmed, releasing her hand as he straightened. 'Is Garstang's sinfully expensive enough for you?'

The exclusive restaurant wasn't one that Darci had ever been to—a junior doctor's pay didn't exactly run to establishments that didn't even list the prices on their menu!—but she had heard of it, of course, and Grant had been there several times, she knew.

'It sounds perfect,' she accepted.

'I'll call for you—'

'No, I'll meet you at the restaurant at eight o'clock,' Darci told him firmly; having this man arrange to pick her up was not part of her plan at all.

Garstang's exclusivity, and the fact that Luc Gambrelli was perfectly confident about being able to secure a booking in a top-class venue that was totally booked months in advance, made it the perfect venue for the humiliation Darci intended to inflict.

She could just picture him now, sitting at the table in the fashionably exclusive Garstang's, looking oh-so-lethally attractive as he waited for her to arrive.

As he waited.

And waited.

Until it finally dawned on him that Darci had no intention of turning up.

That the legendary lover Luc Gambrelli had been publicly stood up.

Sinfully delicious!

CHAPTER THREE

'ARE you sure you don't want to come to the party with Michael and me?' Kerry paused at the door, on her way out to meet her fiancé for the evening.

'Perfectly sure.' Darci grinned at her flatmate reassuringly as she sat on the sofa wearing an old and comfortable pair of pyjamas and wrapped in her duvet. 'I have the evening off, my favourite DVD—' she held it up '—and a bowl of toffee popcorn; what more could I possibly need?'

'Luc Gambrelli?' Kerry suggested provokingly.

'Forget it!' Darci protested.

'Doesn't it bother you at *all* that you could actually be out with him this evening, instead of sitting at home alone eating popcorn and watching a film you've already seen a dozen times before?' Kerry sounded incredulous.

'Not in the least,' Darci assured her smugly. 'Just sitting here imagining Luc Gambrelli waiting at a table in Garstang's for me to arrive is enough to make my evening.'

Kerry looked troubled. 'You agreed that you would call the restaurant and let him know you weren't going to turn up,' she reminded her reprovingly.

Yes, as a concession to Kerry's worrying the last two days

Darci had agreed to do that. She just hadn't said *when* she would do it!

Twenty, even twenty-five minutes past eight o'clock should do it, she had decided. Long enough for the egotistical Luc Gambrelli to be made to feel decidedly uncomfortable at the curious glances of the other diners and the restaurant staff that were sure to be directed his way as it became more and more obvious, as the minutes slowly ticked by, that his date for the evening wasn't going to turn up.

'Stop worrying, Kerry. I *will* call the restaurant and make my excuses,' Darci promised.

'Dammit, I forgot to tell you!' Kerry exclaimed. 'Mellie phoned earlier. She wanted to know how Grant's premiere went on Thursday.'

Darci frowned. 'She did?'

'Stop looking so worried, Darce,' her friend replied. 'I wasn't stupid enough to tell her what you're up to.'

'Good.' Darci breathed her relief.

'Although I probably should have done,' Kerry continued. 'I'm sure Mellie would be the first person to tell you to just let this go.'

'I *am* letting it go,' Darci rejoined. 'Do stop worrying, Kerry! After tonight I don't expect to hear from Luc Gambrelli ever again.'

Kerry raised her eyes heavenwards. 'Let's hope not.'

'Just go, and let me enjoy my movie and my popcorn,' Darci told her friend laughingly, as Kerry still hesitated in the doorway.

She heaved a genuine sigh of relief when her flatmate finally complied. Although Darci had a feeling that Kerry might be right when it came to how Mellie would feel about her interference where Luc Gambrelli was concerned…

Oh, well, it was too late now—and she really did intend to stay well away from the Sicilian in future.

She wait until half past eight before telephoning Garstang's and asking them to pass a message on to Luc Gambrelli that she wasn't well and so wouldn't be able to meet him after all, hastily refusing the offer of having Mr Gambrelli brought to the telephone so that she might tell him that herself; she didn't want to even hear that sexily persuasive voice again!

But that didn't mean that she hadn't thought about Luc Gambrelli a lot over the last two days—that she hadn't remembered the delicious shiver that had run down her spine as his lips had brushed across the back of her hand, and how her body had responded as he'd detailed how he would like to make love to her, while all the time that devilish sense of humour had glinted in his eyes.

And she had guilty thoughts of him right now, as he sat in the restaurant, waiting for her to arrive, probably under the increasingly pitying gazes of the other customers. Thoughts that kept intruding as she tried to watch her favourite film…

It was only the memory of the way Luc Gambrelli had so callously hurt Mellie that made Darci so certain she had been right to carry out her plan to stand him up tonight. The man simply didn't have the right to go around breaking women's hearts without even a backward glance. And especially when that woman was a friend of Darci's.

Then why did she feel so increasingly uncomfortable about what she had done?

It was ridiculous.

Luc Gambrelli deserved everything he got!

When the doorbell rang, a little after nine o'clock, Darci knew she was relieved at the interruption in her tortuous thoughts. She didn't in the least mind pausing the DVD to go and answer the door—any visitor would be a welcome diversion.

Until she opened the door and found that visitor was Luc Gambrelli...

Darci gaped at him, rendered totally speechless as she took in how suavely handsome he looked, in a black silk shirt and black tailored trousers worn beneath a tan suede jacket. The latter was almost a perfect match for his overlong, burnished gold hair, and the shirt and trousers gave the strong angles of his face and his superbly moulded mouth a slightly saturnine appearance.

All of it succeeded in making Darci feel completely vulnerable, dressed as she was in men's striped cotton pyjamas, with her face completely bare of make-up, her hair tousled and her feet bare!

Her legs were in danger of buckling beneath her, she discovered, and she quickly put out a hand to clasp tightly onto the door, the panicky palpitations she could feel in her chest bringing a deep blush to her cheeks.

'I— What— How—' She was gabbling like an idiot, Darci recognised disgustedly. 'What are you doing here?' She finally managed to string a whole sentence together.

Luc took in Darci's appearance in one sweeping glance: her tumbling hair, her flushed face, fevered green eyes. His gaze narrowed as he noted the men's pyjamas she wore and wondered to whom they had originally belonged...

He shrugged broad shoulders. 'I was concerned about you after receiving your message at the restaurant you weren't well,' he responded. 'So I telephoned Grant and asked him for your address.'

Those green eyes widened. 'And he just gave it to you?'

'Why would he not?' Luc replied.

'Well, because—because—' She gave an incredulous shake of her head.

'Once I had explained to him that the two of us should have been having dinner together this evening he was quite happy to be accommodating,' Luc assured her smoothly. 'May I come in?'

'I— Well— Yes, I suppose so,' she accepted grudgingly as she moved back from the door.

Luc stepped inside, noting the crumpled duvet on the sofa before turning back to look at Darci. 'The *maître d'* at Garstang's informed me that you have a fever.'

'Yes,' Darci confirmed, hoping the warmth she could feel in her cheeks looked convincing.

Because Luc Gambrelli was a totally disturbing presence in what she had always considered her private sanctum!

He seemed so big—he was well over six feet to her five feet nine inches—and he made the sitting-room seem somehow smaller, his steel-muscled body totally dominating and exuding a power, a barely restrained strength, that caused a rivulet of apprehension to skitter down the length of Darci's spine.

Did he really believe she was ill? Or was his being here some form of retribution on his part for leaving him sitting in the restaurant all that time?

'Have you consulted a doctor?' he demanded to know.

'I am a doctor,' Darci informed him, and was rewarded by the raising of dark blond brows as he widened those choco-late-brown eyes.

She hadn't expected—not in her wildest dreams!—that Luc would actually turn up at her apartment this way after she had stood him up. If she had, she would have kept the door locked and barricaded herself in her bedroom until he went away again!

But she had stopped shaking now, and while her heart was still beating far too wildly in her chest, the palpitations had thankfully ceased.

All she had to do was reassure Luc that her illness wasn't a hospital case, and then maybe he would leave.

He *had* to leave!

Because just having him here in her apartment was more unsettling, more disturbing, than anything she had ever known in her life. The overhead light was making his hair appear silkily soft in contrast to the harder planes of his aristocratic face. It was enough to overwhelm a woman's senses—*any* woman's senses!—completely.

In fact, Darci wasn't sure she *didn't* have a fever, after all!

She was definitely more aware of Luc Gambrelli, more physically aware of him, than she had a right to be...

'And what is your diagnosis?' Luc persisted, slightly surprised—although why he should be he had no idea—at her choice of profession.

But, in his defence, no doctor he had ever consulted, on the rare occasions that he'd been ill, had *ever* looked like Darci Wilde.

In fact, he would have thought that just facing all that wild red hair, those come-to-bed green eyes, the full pout of her mouth and the temptation of her full, thrusting breasts across the desk in a doctor's consulting room would be enough to raise any man's temperature!

As his own was rising now, as he realised that she wore absolutely nothing beneath those striped pyjamas...

As garments, they shouldn't have been in the least sexy. They were obviously meant for someone much bigger in size—the shoulders hanging loose and the sleeves falling over the slenderness of her hands, and the trousers only held in place by the tie-string at her slender waist as they bagged about her hips. With their awful green-and-cream striped pattern, the pyjamas should have been anything but sexually alluring. But the low neckline of the jacket revealed the slenderness of Darci's throat and a creamy expanse of her bare breasts as they thrust pertly, her nipples taut, against the cotton material.

Luc could imagine nothing more erotic than slowly undoing the buttons down the front of the pyjama jacket to reveal those thrusting breasts, then lavishing the full attention of his lips and tongue across her hardened nipples...

'My diagnosis?' Darci echoed, moistening her lips before replying, although she was slightly disconcerted as Luc's dark gaze followed the movement. 'I have the start of a cold, I believe,' she dismissed briskly, in an effort to dispel the air of—of—*intimacy* that slowly seemed to be surrounding the two of them.

Where was the cautious Kerry, the worrier, when Darci most needed her?

Although after Kerry's anxiety over the last two days, she had a feeling her friend might have little sympathy with Darci's present predicament. Especially as it was completely self-inflicted! Kerry, without having even met Luc Gambrelli, had warned Darci against interfering, seeming to know instinctively that it would be dangerous to wake this sleeping tiger.

It was a pity that Darci's instincts hadn't been as acute!

And that she hadn't thought to pre-warn Grant that under no circumstances was he to reveal her address to Luc Gambrelli....

But it had never occurred to Darci, as she'd made her fiendish plan to leave Luc Gambrelli sitting at Garstang's, that he would actually feel concerned enough about her supposed ill-health to actually seek her out!

The man was completely unpredictable, she decided.

'As I'm sure you appreciate,' she went on firmly, 'there's no actual cure for the common cold, and it's also highly contagious. In fact, I don't think you should even be here in the same room with me,' she added, belatedly registering the intensity of his dark gaze as it roamed freely across her face and body.

Luc gave a slight smile as he recognised her skittishness for exactly what it was. 'But I couldn't possibly desert you when you aren't well,' he drawled huskily. 'Do you live here alone?' he probed, having thought it was rather a large apartment for just one person.

He wondered if the owner of the pyjamas didn't live here, too... Although he would have thought Grant would be more circumspect about telling him of Darci's living arrangements if that were the case...

'My flatmate has gone out this evening,' Darci informed him. 'I have two flatmates, actually, but one of them is away at the moment,' she finished.

Luc quirked blond brows. 'Male or female?'

'Both female, of course,' she came back tartly. 'Now, I really do think you should leave, Luc—'

'And *I* think that you need someone to take care of you— at least until your flatmate returns,' he cut in decisively as he slipped his jacket off and laid it across one of the chairs. 'Point me in the direction of the kitchen and I'll get you something cold to drink. It's important to keep up your liquids when you have a fever, isn't it?' he opined, when she looked totally nonplussed.

Darci couldn't answer him for several seconds, totally

thrown by the expanse of his broad back in the black silk shirt, and by how his muscles rippled beneath the softness of the material.

She had no idea how much time Luc necessarily spent behind a desk for his work, but he obviously made time to work out in a gym: his shoulders were wide and powerful, his chest muscles, and his stomach lean and flat.

In fact, all that lean maleness took her breath away!

Maybe she did have a fever? It would certainly explain the symptoms she was exhibiting: shortness of breath, fevered brow, flushed cheeks and a dry throat.

But she had a feeling that sexual awareness would also explain her ailments—the aching, heavy feeling of her breasts, and the moist heat gathering between her thighs!

She swallowed hard. 'There really is no need for you to stay, Luc. I was about to go to bed anyway—' She broke off, her eyes wide, and gave Luc an awkward glance for what she had just said.

Luc gave a knowing smile at her obvious discomfort. 'Surely, Darci, you don't imagine that I'm about to take advantage of your weakened state?' he mocked softly, all the time knowing that was *exactly* what he had been thinking of doing!

In fact, he seemed to have thought of nothing else, anticipated nothing else, but taking this woman to bed for the last two days. The memory of those challenging green eyes, her temptingly full lips and the lush promise of her body had intruded into his thoughts all too often during the last forty-eight hours.

Finding her here wearing nothing but those disreputable pyjamas was doing absolutely nothing for his tenuous restraint!

'Of course not,' she dismissed sharply, her moss-green

gaze no longer meeting his. 'I—You'll find some juice in the fridge in the kitchen.' Reluctantly, she pointed him in the right direction.

In keeping with the Georgian building in which the flat was housed, the kitchen was long and rambling, with a large work-table in its centre and a breakfast bar at one end, at which it was possible to sit and eat. The room was obviously normally at the centre of life in this spacious apartment. The pots and pans hanging on one wall showed evidence of frequent use, along with the dried herbs set next to the Aga range, for adding to each dish as it was prepared.

A capable cook himself when there was the need, Luc could easily envisage cooking a meal in here with Darci—with or without the pyjamas.

Preferably without!

His body hardened just at the thought of a naked Darci moving effortlessly around the kitchen as they prepared a meal together, at the image of the fullness of her naked breasts, and those lean hips and thighs with a triangle of fiery red hair at their apex...

Having arrived at Garstang's on time this evening, he had been at first irritated, then worried, when Darci hadn't arrived at the restaurant at the appointed time. Then the pendulum had swung to anger as the minutes had ticked by with no sign of her arrival nor a telephone call to explain her tardiness.

It had been almost a relief when James, the *maître d'* had approached his table with the message that Darci had telephoned and was unable to join him after all because she wasn't well.

Almost...

Because Luc hadn't been fooled for a minute by the telephone message. In fact, he was sure that James hadn't been, either. The surprised look in the other man's eyes had been in complete contrast to his politely bland expression! Luc knew that if Darci had really been ill, she would have telephoned the restaurant much earlier than she had to inform him she wasn't able to join him.

Which meant she had to have deliberately left him waiting at the table in Garstang's.

The question was, *why* had she?

Luc had been a little taken aback two evenings ago when Darci had made it a condition of their date that he take her somewhere sinfully expensive if he wanted her to meet him at all. The fact that she then hadn't even bothered to turn up had intrigued him enough for him to take the unprecedented step of contacting Grant in order to ask for his sister's address.

Grant's surprise that his sister and Luc were actually supposed to be out on a date together this evening had been even more interesting, and posed the question *why* hadn't Darci informed her twin on Thursday evening that she had agreed to have dinner with Luc tonight?

Luc had a lot of questions where Darci Wilde was concerned.

Questions, one way or another, he was determined to have answers to…

CHAPTER FOUR

'DRINK some of this. It will make you feel better.'

Darci, sitting cross-legged on the sofa, turned frowningly to take the glass of orange juice from Luc's long tapered fingers, feeling like a fraud at his unexpected display of kindness.

Who would have thought that the heartless Luc Gambrelli, after having been informed Darci wasn't well, would actually come here like this and offer to care for her until Kerry returned later this evening?

Darci certainly hadn't.

It didn't exactly fit in with her image of him as a selfish playboy, did it? she acknowledged, a troubled frown creasing her brow as she sipped the cold juice.

Maybe—

'I also brought you this,' Luc murmured, before placing something against her forehead.

That 'something' was several ice cubes wrapped in cling film which, once placed against Darci's forehead, made her arch up in surprise. Her back stiffened as the intense cold was almost painful against her overheated skin.

'Good grief!' she gasped breathlessly, and she struggled to sit up—the action made harder because of the way she was sitting cross-legged. Her awkwardness dislodged the make-shift ice-pack and caused the cling film to burst open and scatter the ice cubes.

Most of them down the front of Darci's pyjama jacket!

'Oh, dear,' Luc said ruefully as Darci, her entangled legs making it difficult for her to stand up, flapped the pyjama jacket in an effort to stop the icy cubes coming into contact with her flesh. The movement gave Luc, as he stood behind the sofa, tantalising glimpses of her bared breasts...

They were firm and uptilting, their nipples rose-pink, hard and enticing, causing his own flesh to burn, to stiffen, as his body responded.

Luc took a step around the sofa. 'Would you like me to—?'

'Don't even think about it!' Darci cut in warningly as she finally managed to stand up, allowing half a dozen ice cubes to fall onto the carpeted floor as she backed away from him. 'You did that on purpose!' she accused furiously, her cheeks flushed, her green eyes sparkling.

Much as they would look when she was sexually rather than emotionally aroused...

'I was merely trying to help, Darci,' he contradicted. Her pyjama jacket was damp in several places now, the wetness of the material clinging to her luscious curves...

'By almost giving me a heart attack?' she scorned. 'I don't think so!'

Luc didn't think so, either, having considered, as he took the ice cubes out of the freezer to put into her drink, that perhaps a cold awakening was the least Darci deserved for what he was now convinced had been a deliberate ploy on her part to stand him up this evening.

Since arriving at her apartment, Luc had noted the look of

absolute horror on Darci's face when she'd opened the door and found him standing there, had taken in at a glance the almost empty bowl of popcorn in the sitting-room and the fact that the DVD player was on 'Pause', and had become convinced that Darci was no more ill than he was! Before he'd arrived she had obviously been lying on the sofa indulging herself by watching a movie and eating popcorn. Toffee popcorn, he had noted irrelevantly.

The fact that she had decided to continue with the deception of her supposed illness had brought out a need for retribution in him. Hence the deliberately precarious cling film wrap on the ice cubes...

'Now, why on earth would you even suggest that I should deliberately cause those ice cubes to fall?' he asked with feigned innocence.

Darci didn't know—surely Luc couldn't have guessed that her excuse about being ill in order to avoid their date this evening had been a complete fabrication?—she was only sure that he had.

'Because— Well, because—' She broke off as Luc took another step towards her, taking a step back herself as she easily read the intent in those dark, compelling eyes.

Luc Gambrelli was going to kiss her!

'I told you not to even think about it!' she warned sharply as, her gaze fixed on his, she continued to back away—only to come to an abrupt halt as her back hit the wall.

Leaving her trapped by the obviously determined Luc Gambrelli.

'Stay away from me,' she told him breathlessly, eyes wide with apprehension as he continued to move stealthily towards her.

Like the stalking predator he was…

'Are you sure that's what you really want, Darci?' he questioned, and he took the two steps that brought him to stand dangerously close to her.

Darci wasn't sure of anything any more—except that she didn't dare allow Luc Gambrelli to kiss her.

Because, against all reasoning, all her inner warnings that this man was a consummate flirt, as well as being a selfish playboy, she *wanted* him to kiss her!

Her body ached with wanting to feel his hard sculptured lips against hers, her nipples were tingling with awareness, and her inner thighs were warm—becoming warmer by the second!

'I didn't think so, Darci,' he said, his gaze steadily holding hers as he reached out to smooth her hair back over her shoulders, before stroking his fingertips from the hollows at the base of her throat down to the valley between her breasts.

She couldn't breathe—had forgotten how to breathe!—as the touch of those lean, caressing fingers seemed to burn against her flesh. She was completely mesmerised as Luc's head slowly lowered to hers and he claimed her lips with his—gently, softly, enticingly—sipping from her lips, parting them with the tip of his tongue. The hardness of his thighs, pressed intimately against hers, told her of his own arousal…

Darci had no idea what was happening to her as her body curved weakly into his, was only aware that in Luc's arms she had become someone different, someone she didn't recognise. Her body felt full and lush, her breasts and thighs sensitive to his pressing demand, all of her senses now screaming for his intimate touch.

As his lips became heated on hers, as he deepened this kiss and his hand moved to cup beneath one throbbing breast, his thumb stroking unerringly across the hardened tip, Darci forgot everything and everyone else, able only to feel and taste Luc.

Her hands were crushed against his chest, against warm skin and solid muscle, and every inch of him was hard male as his mouth continued to plunder and capture hers, his tongue seeking out every secret as it probed and caressed and duelled with hers. Her throat arched instinctively as he broke that kiss to trail moist kisses against that sensitive column, down to the creamy swell of her breasts, his hands now busy with the buttons down the front of her pyjama jacket.

He looked up, his gaze easily holding hers captive as he peeled the sides of the jacket back, his eyes darkening appreciatively as he finally looked down at the naked fullness of her breasts.

'You're beautiful,' he groaned achingly, and his head lowered.

Darci barely had time to draw in a ragged breath before his mouth closed moistly over one turgid nipple, drawing its fullness into his warmth as his tongue licked and stroked its ultra-sensitive tip and his other hand captured its twin, to caress and roll the peak between his fingertips. Waves of restless need washed over her as she felt herself swelling, as hot moisture pulsed between her thighs.

Luc had never tasted anything, anyone, as delicious as Darci. Her breast was pure nectar as he drank his fill of her with his lips and tongue, as he laved her nipple, sucking harder on that dusky tip as she held his head cradled against her and he heard her throaty groans of pleasure.

He continued to suckle her breast as his hand moved to the tie on her pyjama bottoms, deftly releasing the bow to let them fall to the floor so that he might touch the flesh beneath, seeking, caressing, gently cupping her there. He was able to feel her fiery heat, her dampness, her legs parting as she completely opened herself to him.

Her hands moved up to grasp his shoulders as he made his claim on her heat, stroking those soft, moist lips so that she arched against him.

She was on fire with need, Darci acknowledged, as she moved to allow Luc greater access between her legs. Her neck arched, thrusting her breast into his mouth as he entered her with first one finger and then two. His thumb sought out the hard nub above and he stroked her to a sobbing release that caught her and carried her over the edge of an abyss, as wave after wave of heat and sensation made her body pulse and contract in pure pleasure.

That sobbing release turned to genuine distress as reality hit her like a tidal wave. As she realised in whose arms she was, whose caressing hands had been on and in her body only seconds ago.

Her lids were heavy as she raised them to look up at Luc Gambrelli. The dark glitter of his eyes and the flush to his cheeks told of his own arousal.

An unfulfilled arousal.

Darci pulled away from him to hold the two sides of the pyjama top across her breasts and thighs, her legs still shaking from the force of her release.

'Are you okay?' Luc prompted huskily, as he saw her inner struggle to accept what had just happened between them.

He hadn't meant for things to go quite as far as they had—had meant only to demonstrate to Darci how futile it was for her to try to avoid being with him the way she had earlier this evening.

Instead of just doing that he had become carried away—

with Darci's arousal, as well as his own. Unable to resist touching her, caressing her, unable to resist being inside her as her body exploded and convulsed in release.

A surrender that had only made her distrust of him deepen, if the fury snapping in her eyes and the look of self-disgust on her face were anything to go by!

He drew in a controlling breath as he fought down the clamouring of his own body. 'What just happened was inevitable, Darci—'

'Maybe to you it was,' she returned scathingly, as she quickly rebuttoned her top. 'But not to me!'

If Darci sought to return some semblance of propriety to this conversation by covering herself, then she was achieving the opposite, Luc acknowledged ruefully, noting that Darci's long legs were still enticingly naked beneath the thigh-length garment.

'What do you do in circumstances like this, Luc?' she challenged him. 'Give yourself half a notch on the bedpost rather than one?'

He looked at her darkly. 'I don't think insulting me is going to help this situation—'

'You think that was insulting?' she came back shrilly. 'Let me assure you, Luc, where you're concerned, I haven't even begun!'

'No one forced you into responding, dammit!' Luc lost his temper, the ache in his own arousal—his unfulfilled arousal!—still throbbing painfully.

'Oh, I might have known you would throw that in my face!' Darci came back furiously. 'But what chance did I have of refusing when the great lover, the practised seducer Luc Gambrelli, decided to turn all his considerable expertise onto me!'

'I would advise you to stop right there, Darci,' Luc bit out forcefully, a nerve pulsing in his tightly clenched jaw, his eyes blazing with his own leashed temper.

'Why should I?' Darci defied him. 'You just had to prove that you can have any woman you please, didn't you? Couldn't accept that there might be any woman in the universe who isn't impressed by the legendary Luc Gambrelli—'

'I told you to stop, Darci!' he warned between gritted teeth.

'And you expect me to obey, too, don't you?' she rejoined. 'Well, welcome to the real world, Luc—you're the last man, the *very* last man, I would ever obey—either now or in the future!'

Luc stilled at her vehemence, his gaze narrowing on her searchingly as he tried to make sense of everything that had happened since he'd first met her.

Was it possible that her coolness towards him on Thursday evening had been a deliberate ploy to engage his attention?

That her elusiveness when he'd asked her out had been just as deliberate?

As had her demand that he take her somewhere sinfully expensive?

Had she done those things with the intention of just as deliberately leaving him sitting alone in Garstang's for half an hour before telephoning to let him know she wouldn't be joining him after all?

Was it possible that she had never had any intention of keeping their date?

It was possible—more than possible!—yes.

But Luc had no idea why.

Even less so after the way she had responded to him just now....

Although that response was obviously something Darci

deeply regretted, and unfortunately it only seemed to have added fuel to whatever resentment she had already been feeling towards him.

But Luc couldn't fathom why it was she felt that resentment. He knew that he had never met Darci before—he would certainly have remembered her if he had!

Neither could it have anything to do with her brother Grant; he and the other man had worked well together on the film *Turning Point*, and had already discussed collaborating on another project in several months' time.

So what had caused Darci's resentment?

'Tell me, Darci,' he purred, deceptively softly, 'what have I done that has—upset you in this way?'

Darci gave him a startled look, realising that in her agitation—in her self-disgust at her own weakness towards this man!—she had probably revealed too much. The last thing she wanted to do was betray her friend's confidence by revealing just how badly Luc had hurt Mellie six weeks ago.

'Isn't making love to me just now enough to be going on with?' she came back indignantly.

'No,' he replied calmly. 'Because your attitude dates back to before that,' he added confidently.

Darci moistened dry lips, wishing she were in a more advantageous position than she was—that she at least had all her clothes on! 'That's nonsense, Luc—'

'No, it isn't,' he contradicted smoothly, that dark gaze narrowed speculatively.

'Of course it is,' she defended. 'You said you came here this evening out of concern because I was ill, and instead—'

'You are no more ill than I am, Darci,' he cut in hardly. 'I can assure you, you are in robust health!'

Very robust health if her memory of her reaction to his hardened body pressed so intimately against hers was anything to go by!

And she was sure that it was. Her legs felt weak just at the thought of that hard, muscled body against hers, her cheeks hot as she recalled the touch of those sensuous lips and tongue against her breasts, the way she had opened herself to him as his hand intimately caressed her.

The way her inner thighs still ached from the force of her physical release…!

As Kerry had pointed out so bluntly three days ago, Darci had been far too busy for relationships these last ten years, only having allowed herself the occasional date with a colleague as a break from her rigid regime. Obviously all those years of abstinence had done Darci absolutely no good whatsoever if she could respond so wantonly to Luc Gambrelli, a man who had hurt and betrayed one of her best friends!

'I have no idea what you're talking about, Luc,' she told him dismissively, stepping out of her fallen pyjama bottoms to move across the room. 'I would like you to leave now, if you don't mind,' she added hardly, the crumpled lower garment a stark reminder of the fact that she had been almost completely naked in this man's arms a few minutes ago, while *he* was still fully dressed—and looking slightly satanic with it!—in black shirt and trousers.

Luc drew in a harsh breath, knowing there was much more to Darci's behaviour over the last few days than she obviously intended sharing with him.

Yet.

Because he had no intention of just walking away from Darci this evening and never seeing her again; he intended getting to the bottom of her resentment towards him if he could. He was absolutely certain now that she had felt resentment towards him before he had even spoken to her on Thursday evening.

He gave a terse inclination of his head. 'I think that might be advisable—for now.'

'For now?' she echoed warily.

Luc gave a humourless smile. 'I don't like mysteries, Darci—and I find your behaviour a puzzle verging upon an enigma!'

'I can't imagine why.' She gave an impatient shake of her head. 'Just accept that there's one woman who doesn't go weak at the knees just looking at you—'

'All evidence is to the contrary, Darci,' he drawled mockingly, and was rewarded by a flash of fiery anger that coloured her cheeks and made her eyes sparkle accusingly.

He knew he was behaving like a complete bastard by reminding her of her weakness a short time ago, but that interlude, pleasuring her, was the only evidence he had that Darci was keeping something from him—something that made her deny even her own response to him. A response she would dearly have liked to pretend had never happened, if that mutinous glitter in her eyes was anything to go by.

But, at the same time, she knew that even if she could forget it, Luc had no intention of doing so....

He grimaced. 'I don't believe we will achieve anything by discussing this…situation any further this evening, Darci—'

'We aren't going to discuss this any further at all!'

'We will have dinner together tomorrow evening—'

'We most certainly will not!' she assured him incredulously.

'Oh, yes,' he asserted, 'we will. But not in a restaurant this time,' he stated forcefully. 'Instead I will bring the makings of our dinner here, leaving it to you to ensure that your flat-mates have gone out.'

'I said we *aren't* having dinner together, Luc,' Darci told him frustratedly. 'Not tomorrow or any other time!'

He quirked one blond, arrogant brow. 'You would rather that we continue this…discussion…in front of your flatmates?'

'I don't intend continuing this discussion at all, let alone in front of any third party,' Darci snapped impatiently.

He gave an arrogant smile. 'Nevertheless, I will be here at seven-thirty tomorrow evening. It is your choice whether or not your flatmates are present.'

'Flatmate,' Darci corrected him sharply. 'I told you that one of my flatmates is away at the moment,' she reminded him.

Mellie—the woman this man had used and then so callously discarded, Darci reminded herself vehemently.

As Luc would no doubt discard Darci herself once he had satisfied his curiosity about her….

'So you did.' He nodded unconcernedly. 'Until tomorrow evening, then, Darci.' He bent to pick up his jacket, shrugging his broad shoulders into it before turning to look at her from between narrowed lids. 'My advice, despite what you may feel to the contrary, is for you not to absent yourself tomorrow evening,' he told her hardly. 'That would only involve my having to contact Grant again in order to ascertain your where-abouts…' he explained.

Darci stared at him impotently. All Kerry's warnings about the wisdom of attempting to inflict retribution on Luc Gambrelli for hurting Mellie seemed to have come true.

Grant was going to be curious enough about her date with Luc Gambrelli this evening, and would no doubt tease her mercilessly about not confiding in him about it. She had to avoid adding fuel to that fire by allowing Luc to talk to Grant about her again.

She glared. 'I dislike you intensely, Mr Gambrelli!' she told him fiercely.

He gave a slow, deliberate smile as his gaze moved slowly up the long length of her bare legs, over her thighs and slender waist, before coming to rest warmly on the firm thrust of her breasts.

Breasts that instantly betrayed her when her nipples hardened against the material of her top!

'Yes, I can see that you do,' he observed knowingly, before strolling unconcernedly to the door. 'Until tomorrow evening, Darci,' he repeated over his shoulder, before quietly letting himself out of the flat.

Darci stared after him.

She wanted to throw something.

Wanted to hit something.

Wanted to scream and shout.

And all to no avail. She knew doing any of those things would make absolutely no difference to the outcome of her conversation with Luc Gambrelli. She had no choice—unless she wanted Grant to become even more involved than he already was, which she most certainly didn't!—but to prepare herself for Luc Gambrelli to arrive back here at seven-thirty tomorrow evening....

CHAPTER FIVE

THE snug-fitting denims and green T-shirt Darci was wearing the following evening, when she opened the door to Luc's ring on the doorbell prompt at seven-thirty, were, he considered, a vast improvement on the striped pyjamas she had been wearing the night before. This outfit emphasised the feline leanness of her body beneath the full swell of her breasts.

Although Luc couldn't say he approved of the fact that Darci had swept back all that fiery-red hair and secured it in a loose topknot that dulled its colour to auburn.

However, the mutinous sparkle in those moss-green eyes as she looked at him in challenge warned Luc not to say anything that would put tinder to that particular flame.

He smiled enigmatically as he strolled past her into the apartment. 'I think we should open this right now.' He pulled a bottle of red wine from the bag he carried. 'You look in need of a glass,' he opined dryly.

'I already have a bottle of red wine open in the kitchen,' Darci told him tersely. Never usually one for drinking on her own, she'd felt she needed a glass this evening, in order to fortify her nerves ready for when Luc Gambrelli arrived.

In view of the fact that he was dressed much less formally

than when she had previously seen him—his own faded denims fitting low down on his lean hips, the black fitted T-shirt emphasising his flat, muscled stomach and the powerful width of his shoulders providing a sharp contrast to the burnished gold of his overlong hair—her instinct had obviously been a correct one!

'Are we alone this evening?' he enquired mildly as he placed a laden bag down on the table that stood in the middle of the kitchen.

Darci's gaze narrowed. She knew he was asking if she had complied with his advice and asked Kerry not to be here.

As it happened, she hadn't needed to ask Kerry to go out—because once Kerry had arrived home the night before, and Darci had told her of her own disastrous evening, her friend had felt absolutely no inclination to be here when Luc Gambrelli came back again tonight. In fact, Kerry had opted out of the situation altogether, and decided to spend the night at Michael's flat!

'Yes,' she confirmed tersely, her eyes widening slightly as Luc took prawns, steaks, mushrooms, baby potatoes and the makings of a salad from the bag he had carried in with him. 'I really don't think I'm going to be able to eat any of that,' she told him, as she poured some of the red wine into a glass for him and topped up her own at the same time.

He looked at her curiously. 'I should warn you, Darci, I do not intend to go hungry again this evening,' he told her, as he lifted the glass and took a sip of wine.

Darci felt cross. 'I don't believe for a moment that you went without dinner last night—'

'I wasn't necessarily referring to food,' Luc corrected her, raising one mocking brow as Darci eyed him suspiciously.

She delivered him a quelling glance as his meaning became clear. 'Let's get one thing straight, shall we, Luc?' she bit out tensely.

'By all means,' he drawled, as he leant back against the table to look at her with calm enquiry.

Her mouth thinned. 'I am not one of those aspiring young actresses in Los Angeles who are just so grateful to have you even notice them that they are more than willing to share your bed! Neither am I impressed by the legendary lover, Luc Gambrelli—'

'That appears to be two things, Darci,' Luc cut in dangerously, not liking the way this conversation was shaping up at all. 'And that's one more time in our acquaintance that you've referred to me as a "legendary lover"—in a derogatory way,' he pointed out.

'Because that's what you are!' Darci told him impatiently. 'The newspapers are constantly full of stories about the relationships that you, your brother and your cousin—'

'Both Wolf and Cesare are now happily married and completely faithful to their respective wives,' he pointed out.

'That just means that, as the only single Gambrelli male left, the press will concentrate completely on your own exploits in future,' Darci retaliated.

Luc was well aware of that. Just as he was aware that for the last three months, since the shock of Wolf's marriage so soon after Cesare's, there hadn't been any exploits of his for the newspapers to sensationalise. Unlike his brother and his cousin, Luc had no intention of falling foul of the dreaded Gambrelli Curse: namely, finding himself hopelessly in love, and—worst of all!—married.

He shook his head. 'The tabloid press simply write what the public wants to read,' he dismissed unconcernedly.

That hadn't been true concerning his relationship with Mellie, thank goodness, Darci thought. The last thing Darci would have wanted to read in the newspapers was how this man had broken her friend's heart some weeks ago.

But, again, she couldn't bring Mellie into this without betraying her friend's confidence....

'You're totally missing my point, Luc,' she told him impatiently.

'That point being...?' Once again he quirked that arrogant brow. A gesture that was beginning to irritate Darci immensely.

'That, no matter what you may have assumed to the contrary, I do not go to bed with womanising playboys!'

He took another sip of his wine, not betraying his reaction to her deliberate insult by so much as a twitch of that annoying eyebrow. 'That sounds like a very sensible philosophy to me,' he finally reasoned.

Darci wasn't fooled for a moment by the pleasantness of his tone; she could see the way his eyes had narrowed, and the very stillness of his leanly muscled body was a warning in itself.

A warning she decided not to heed. 'I was referring to *you*!' she told him defiantly, her whole body taut as she waited for his response.

He nodded. 'Yes, I thought you were.' He placed his wineglass down on the kitchen table, his movements slow and deliberate, before turning to walk around the table to where Darci stood, coming to a halt only inches away from her. 'Perhaps, Darci, it would be better if you waited to be *asked* to share my bed before saying no?'

Darci stood her ground, glaring up at him, determined not to be intimidated by his close proximity.

Even if she was!

For all Luc's lazy elegance of movement, his ultra-calm expression, Darci could feel the danger, the threat swirling beneath that stillness, and knew that beneath the trappings of his casual clothing Luc's body was taut with displeasure. Those dark eyes were no longer laughing, but glittering down at her with intent.

This man, she realised with wary clarity, was much more than he appeared on the surface!

Much more than the womanising playboy she had just accused him of being?

Yes, much more, she recognised, as an apprehensive quiver moved across her skin.

At this moment he was more than ever that sleeping tiger she knew she had awakened—and if she didn't tread very carefully she was in danger of getting mauled!

She moistened her lips with the tip of her tongue, instantly stopping the movement when she saw the way Luc's gaze darkened hungrily as it followed the progress of the pink tip of her tongue. Reminding her all too forcefully of the way his tongue had caressed her in the same way the evening before!

She made an impatient movement, thankfully breaking the momentary threat as Luc's gaze returned enquiringly to her own.

'Perhaps we should just cook dinner?' she suggested wearily.

He remained unmoving for several long—tension-filled!—seconds, as his dark eyes roamed shrewdly over the paleness of her face, before he gave a terse inclination of his head and stepped away from her. 'Perhaps we should,' he allowed gruffly. 'I am much…mellower when I have been fed,' he assured her self-derisively. 'Let's hope that the same is also true of you.'

There was an implicit warning in his words that Darci knew

she would be foolish to ignore. Very foolish. And, though she might be many things, foolish certainly wasn't one of them.

Although she wasn't exactly looking forward to coping with a mellower Luc Gambrelli once they had eaten dinner!

Dinner was surprisingly fun to cook—Luc proving himself to be a creative, as well as capable cook as he sautéed the prawns with garlic and then prepared a fresh, creamy mushroom sauce to go with the steak. Darci did the more basic cooking of the meat itself, as well as the potatoes and the preparation of a salad. Luc finished his contribution by preparing a vinegar and mustard dressing to go with the latter.

He sat across the kitchen table from Darci once they had finished eating their meal, looking at her from beneath lowered lids. The room felt comfortably informal, as he had guessed it might the evening before. Darci, he had been pleased to note, had relaxed a little herself as they'd prepared dinner together, showing none of the lack of appetite she had claimed earlier as they ate all the food and drank several more glasses of red wine.

He had been deeply annoyed at their conversation before dinner, but it was an annoyance he recognised as being slightly illogical. Because he knew he had earned his reputation—even if he wouldn't have quite put it in the term of being a womanising playboy!

He certainly didn't like the idea that that was what Darci thought him to be!

He was thirty-four years old, had been sexually active since the age of sixteen and had never married, and so of course there had been women in his life. He didn't regret any of those affairs, either.

Especially when it was the very experience he had gained that had enabled him to give Darci such pleasure the evening before....

'So tell me,' he prompted lazily as they lingered over the cheese course, 'what made you decide to become a doctor?'

He had spent a lot of the time as they prepared dinner together in surreptitiously watching Darci as she worked. He had noted the slenderness of her wrists and her long hands, her economy of movement, and had known that she was the sort of woman who took a pride in doing something well. It was also clear that she would bring the same economy and efficiency of movement to her chosen profession.

And to her lovemaking...?

It was a long time since Luc had fantasised about making love with any woman—since he had needed to!—but as he'd watched Darci he hadn't been able to stop himself from imagining those slender fingers on his body, as she touched and caressed him, and had almost been able to feel her stroking him.

Darci thought awhile, not exactly mellowed by the food she had eaten and the wine she had drunk, but certainly not as tense as she had been earlier, either. Which was due, in part, she knew, to the fact that Luc had been decidedly unthreatening—deliberately so?—as they'd prepared dinner together.

'Why did *you* become a film producer?' she came back dryly.

Luc shook his head. 'It isn't the same. Medicine isn't something you enter into on a whim. It takes dedication and a lot of hard work.'

Darci quirked one auburn brow. 'And is that what you did? Became a film producer on a whim?' she explained, at his questioning look.

She was turning this conversation back on him, Luc knew. In an effort not to talk about herself?

Probably, he acknowledged, recognising that, like him, Darci didn't enjoy talking about her private life. And as a doctor, there to listen to a patient's symptoms before making a diagnosis, she'd get away with keeping her privacy most of the time, too.

No matter. He would allow himself to be diverted for the moment, but when he was ready, they would return to the subject of Darci.

He gave a rueful smile. 'My cousin Cesare owns the Gambrelli chain of hotels, a recording studio and an airline, as well as numerous other business endeavours. My brother, Wolf, is into property ownership and development worldwide, and, as Count Gambrelli, he also deals with the running of the family estates in Italy.' He paused. 'Younger brothers—the "spare", I believe they are called in this country—have a tough time of it trying to find their niche in life.'

Darci gave him a considering look, instinctively knowing that no matter how Luc might choose to make light of it, younger brother or not, he would be good at whatever he chose to do.

Including as a lover…?

Especially as a lover, she accepted, with a hardening of her resolve not to fall under this man's spell.

Something she was in danger of doing now, as the evening progressed—all the time aware of Luc's raw energy beneath that easygoing façade, of the sensual lure of his body, of the muscles that rippled beneath that black T-shirt when he moved. Even the aftershave he wore had invaded her senses….

Possibly, she allowed grudgingly.

Definitely, she admitted self-disgustedly.

She was more aware of Luc Gambrelli—sexually, as well as otherwise—than she had ever been of a man in her life before!

'Well, you certainly found your niche,' she said. 'Both in and out of the film studio,' she added cheekily, and then stood up abruptly and began to clear the table.

Luc watched her, aware that she was trying to antagonise him once again. That something—some thought, perhaps?—had put Darci back on the defensive.

That same defensiveness that had dictated her behaviour towards him on Thursday evening, when they'd first met?

Probably.

But Luc felt less inclined to push for answers about the reasons for her defensiveness now. He knew that once he did, once Darci had told him exactly why it was she distrusted him, she would then ensure they didn't see each other again.

And he wanted to see her again.

Wanted more than that.

Much more.

He wanted to touch her again as he had last night!

But with Darci, he knew, it was going to be a question of waiting, of biding his time, of spending more evenings like this one getting to know her, before attempting to push their relationship onto the more intimate footing that he craved.

He stood up to join her as she loaded the dishwasher. 'You didn't answer my question as to why you became a doctor,' he reminded her.

She barely glanced at him before resuming loading the dishes into the machine. 'I always wanted to be a doctor,' she said flatly.

Luc studied her bent head, his fingers itching to release her hair from its confining clip. He wanted to watch as that fiery thickness cascaded onto her shoulders and down the long length of her back.

It was an impulse he resisted by curling his hands into fists at his sides. 'And do you always get what you want?' he prompted.

Darci straightened to give Luc a long, assessing glance, knowing that at some time in the last few minutes the atmosphere had changed, becoming more intimate, more sexually charged. It was a situation that had to be dispelled as quickly as possible.

Like now!

'Don't you?' she challenged, with barely concealed sarcasm.

He easily returned her gaze. 'Yes, but I would like to think not to anyone else's detriment,' he finally replied.

Not true in Mellie's case, Darci reminded herself determinedly.

Although it was a reminder that was having less and less effect the more time she spent in Luc Gambrelli's company. She suddenly realised that she hadn't given Mellie, or the heartache this man had caused her friend, a single thought as she and Luc had cooked and eaten dinner together.

After telling herself earlier that she wasn't in the least foolish, she now knew it would be the height of foolishness if she were to actually fall for Luc herself!

She straightened. 'It's getting late, Luc, and I have to go into the hospital early in the morning, so I think it's time you left,' she told him impatiently, knowing that her impatience was directed at herself rather than at him. Luc hadn't done anything this evening that she could claim as being in the least deliberately provocative; all of this physical awareness, this intimacy, was coming directly from inside *her*.

Because she remembered so vividly the touch of his hands and lips the night before, had lain awake in her bed last night long after parting from Kerry, unable to sleep as she'd tried, and failed, to put thoughts of Luc Gambrelli's lovemaking from her mind.

Luc watched the emotions chasing across Darci's expressive face as she so obviously fought some sort of inner battle with herself.

Over him?

Lord, he hoped so—he would hate to think he was going to suffer all the physical torture of enforced abstinence alone!

Because it *was* torture not to reach out and take Darci in his arms, to kiss her, touch her, as he so longed to do. As he knew that he couldn't do if he intended being with her again. He knew instinctively that she would use any physical coercion on his part now as a reason not to see him again.

'Of course,' he accepted. 'Perhaps you would have lunch with me on your next day off?'

He was rewarded by Darci's startled look. 'Lunch?' she repeated.

He gave a wry smile. 'It is a meal, usually partaken of at some time between midday and three o'clock—'

'I know what lunch is, Luc,' she cut in. 'I just—I assumed you would be returning to Los Angeles some time during the next few days.'

'Did you?' he mused, his intention having been to go to Paris this week, rather than Los Angeles. Before he had met Darci, that was.

Before he had decided that capturing her, taking her to his bed, was the more urgent of the two….

But, no matter what did or didn't happen between the two

of them in the next few days, he really did have to be in Paris by next weekend. Unless he wanted to incur the wrath of his whole family!

Darci brooded. Well, of course she had thought Luc was returning to America soon. Why wouldn't she?

Luc didn't live in London. He had no home here as far as she was aware—had only come to London for the English premiere of Grant's film, *Turning Point*. So, yes, of course she had assumed Luc would be returning to his life in Los Angeles in the next few days.

It had been that knowledge, she now realised, the thought that he wouldn't have time to see her again, that had helped her get through this evening.

Luc's suggestion that they meet for lunch on her next day off seemed to indicate he felt no immediate urgency to return home at the moment.

'When is your free day, Darci?' he persisted firmly.

'Tuesday,' she answered absently. 'But—'

'Then we will have lunch on Tuesday, yes?'

'No!'

'Why not?' Once again he quirked that expressive brow.

'Because—Luc, I don't like playing games!' she told him agitatedly. 'We've had dinner, as you suggested, now let's just—just stay away from each other, hmm?'

'But we have not, as I also suggested, had our conversation concerning the puzzle of your behaviour towards me since we met on Thursday evening,' he reminded her.

Her deliberate coolness, he meant. Her rudeness, and the fact that she had deliberately not turned up for their dinner date yesterday evening, either, after demanding he take her somewhere sinfully expensive....

It was a conversation Darci would rather they continued to avoid.

'Unless you would care to have that conversation now?' Luc challenged her, as he seemed to read some of her thoughts.

Damn him.

And damn *her*, she mentally berated herself. She should have taken Kerry's advice and just stayed out of this. Now, instead, she found that Luc Gambrelli had invaded her life and was refusing to leave!

She gave a shake of her head. 'I really can't see the point in prolonging this—this acquaintance,' she told him directly.

'No?' Luc said, and he took a step closer to her, reaching up, as he had longed to do all evening, and removing the clip from her hair, freeing the fiery tresses to shimmer like living flame about her shoulders and down her spine. His breath caught in his throat as Darci instantly looked wild and wanton.

Exactly how Luc wanted her!

He slowly lowered his head towards hers, hearing her breath catch in her throat a mere second before his lips gently claimed hers. He drew her lower lip into his mouth, his eyes open and locked with hers as he nibbled sensuously before running his tongue along that inner sensitivity. He was rewarded by Darci's groan of capitulation as her mouth opened to allow him to deepen the kiss, her eyes closing as her arms moved up about his shoulders and her fingers became entangled in the hair at his nape.

She felt so good, tasted so good, that Luc didn't want to stop there. He wanted to pick her up and carry her to her bed, to kiss and caress every velvety inch of her before burying himself deep inside her, stroking her wetness, gliding in and out of her, until he pumped his seed into her and joined her in an earth-shattering climax.

Instead he raised his head reluctantly, and his hands moved to grasp the tops of her arms. He held her away from him, knowing by her slightly unfocused green eyes, the flush to her cheeks, that Darci was as aroused as he was—that she wanted him to do all those things, too.

But Luc knew that anticipation would bring a much greater reward for both of them. He was determined that when he and Darci made love, she wouldn't be able to accuse him of seducing her, that she would come to his bed of her own free will.

'*That* is the point of prolonging this acquaintance,' he explained. 'I will call for you here at one o'clock on Tuesday,' he instructed, then he released her to move determinedly away from her and stride through to the sitting-room.

It took Darci a few seconds to regain her scattered wits before she quickly followed him. 'Luc—'

'Not another word, Darci.' He put silencing fingertips across her lips. 'We have managed to get through this evening without…serious disagreements. Let's leave it that way, hmm?' he added teasingly.

She didn't *want* to leave it that way! Not when leaving it meant he expected her to be waiting here for him on Tuesday when he called for her at one o'clock!

She drew in a ragged breath. 'I really can't—'

'I am not taking no for an answer, Darci,' he informed her briskly. 'Which means it would be advisable for you to actually be here on Tuesday,' he responded dryly.

Darci blinked. 'Or…?'

Luc shrugged. 'I am sure that a call to Grant will supply me with the information as to which hospital you work at, so that I might find you there when you return to work on Wednesday…'

Grant had phoned Darci earlier today, before he went off

on a couple of weeks' location shooting in Bulgaria—or Bolivia. She knew it was somewhere beginning with a *B*! Darci had not in the least appreciated her brother's comment, 'So you were impressed, after all?' in reference to the fact that he knew she had arranged to have dinner with Luc Gambrelli the evening before!

But Grant never went anywhere without his mobile phone—not even this place beginning with *B*—and so would be completely reachable if Luc should need to call him....

And she didn't like to think what the hospital staff, let alone her patients, would make of Luc Gambrelli—this golden-haired Sicilian god!—scouring the hospital looking for the normally serious and highly professional Dr Darci Wilde!

'Lock up after I leave, hmm?' Luc encouraged, as he walked to the door to quietly let himself out.

What was the point in locking up after he left when it was Luc himself that Darci should be barring her door against? she wondered disgruntledly, as she slowly moved to drop the catch on the door.

Because there was no doubt in her mind that Luc Gambrelli was getting to her!

Against everything she knew about him, against every warning her body screamed at her during the rare moments when she wasn't totally befuddled by her complete physical awareness of him, Darci knew that Luc was getting well and truly under her guard.

And, after years of avoiding anything resembling a serious—or a physical—relationship, Darci knew that, even though she was twenty-eight years old, she simply didn't have the experience to guard herself against that invasion.

CHAPTER SIX

'WHERE are we going?'

Luc gave Darci a brief glance from behind his dark sunglasses as she sat beside him in the black sports car that he had borrowed for the day from his cousin Cesare. The soft top was down, and Darci wore her long red tresses unconfined today, so that they tumbled in the wind and gleamed like fire as the sun shone down on the two of them.

Darci had been waiting for Luc at her apartment when he'd arrived just before one o'clock, relieving him of the trouble of having to go looking for her. Something he had considered might be a definite possibility after her stubbornness before he'd left on Sunday evening.

But he should have known that Darci was made of much sterner stuff than that. That she wasn't the sort of woman who would run away and hide from what she had to know was the inevitability of a relationship between the two of them.

At least, he hoped she realised it was inevitable....

The last thirty-six hours had been incredibly long ones as far as Luc was concerned. Most of them had been spent in his suite at the London Gambrelli Hotel as he'd considered his plan of action for taking the elusive Darci Wilde to his or her—it didn't matter which!—bed.

That long drawn-out day and a half had at least brought him to one conclusion: whatever course of action he settled on, it could not include him staying away from Darci for long!

'I am taking you out to lunch,' he answered her confidently as he continued to manoeuvre the car through the suburban London traffic and out into the English countryside.

Darci frowned at him behind her sunglasses. 'Are we going to a country pub?'

'No.'

'A country hotel.'

'No.'

'A golf club with a restaurant, then?' They had to be going somewhere like that, because they were leaving London far behind!

Not a reassuring realisation in the circumstances....

'Again, no,' Luc drawled mockingly.

'A burger joint?' she said, out of desperation.

He shook his head. 'We could have stayed in London for that! But, no, I am afraid I have never understood the liking people have for fast-food restaurants,' he responded.

Neither had Darci—although she had indulged several times while she was in medical school, when she'd been hungry and her time off had been limited.

'Just tell me where we're going, Luc,' she prompted in an impatient tone, knowing that it wasn't helping her slightly resentful mood that Luc looked so damned gorgeous!

His hair shone in the sunshine, and his already olive-complexioned face—that hard-angled face that was so handsome it was almost beautiful—was tanned a deep bronze.

Darci had told herself this morning that his body couldn't really be as hard and muscled as her dreams last night had suggested it was. Only to be proved completely wrong when she'd opened the flat door to him earlier, and the sight of his honed body in tight faded denims and a white T-shirt had rendered her breathless.

Perhaps, she decided, with another sideways glance at him now, Luc was short for Lucifer—because this man tempted her more sinfully than she had ever been tempted before!

'It's a surprise,' he answered her cryptically.

'I don't like surprises,' she shot back.

'Everyone likes surprises, Darci,' he dismissed with a grin, his teeth very white against his bronzed skin.

Not when Luc Gambrelli was generating that surprise, they didn't!

Although Darci had a feeling that when it came to Luc, women and surprises, she was in a minority— probably of one!

Because most women wouldn't *care* that any relationship with Luc was sure to be of short duration—would simply enjoy the affair while it lasted, enjoy *him* while it lasted.

Unfortunately Darci simply wasn't made that way. She had grown up in a loving family, and her parents had been absolutely devoted to each other—they were still. And Darci had promised herself that one day, once she was firmly established in her career, she would have that sort of partnership for herself.

Her plans *didn't* include a deviation into a fling with someone like Luc Gambrelli!

'I don't,' she assured him firmly.

Luc had no doubt that it was in just such a voice that Darci advised her less cooperative patients. Unfortunately for Darci, he wasn't one of them...

'I'm sure that as a child you must have enjoyed the anticipation of Christmas and birthdays?' he persisted.

'Well, of course,' she retorted. 'But neither of us are
children, Luc. And I really can't just disappear from
London like this for hours on end.' She looked at the surrounding countryside as it sped past. 'I may be needed at
the hospital—'

'It is your day off and you're not on call,' he pointed out,
having no intention of turning back now that he had got Darci
all to himself.

'Well…yes,' she accepted grudgingly. 'But I often go in on
my days off.'

'Through choice, or because you are called in?' he queried.

Darci gave a sigh. 'Luc, being a doctor isn't just a nine-
'til-five job. People get sick twenty-four hours a day.'

'In other words, you go in because you want to?' Luc
guessed. 'And all work and no play makes you a stressed and
less-than-efficient Darci.'

She glared at him over the top of her sunglasses. 'I thought
the saying was—"makes Jack a dull boy"?'

A glare Luc chose to ignore. 'So I used a little poetic
licence.' He grinned. 'My point being,' he continued firmly,
when he could see she was about to protest again, 'that you
and your patients will benefit from your taking time off away
from the hospital to have some fun.'

'Luc—'

'This will do,' he decided imperiously, and he turned the car
off into a wooded parkland area, hoping Cesare would forgive
him for the effect the uneven dirt road was having on the sus-
pension of the Porsche, but knowing, once he had explained
the situation to his cousin, that Cesare would understand.

And if, in his newly respectable married state, Cesare didn't understand, then Luc would simply replace the Porsche!

Fun! The word Luc had used for today echoed mockingly in Darci's brain.

She wasn't having fun! She was so tense, what with her complete awareness of Luc, so churned-up inside, that she couldn't breathe properly, let alone think. She certainly wasn't having *fun*!

And now Luc had turned the car off into a forest area miles from anywhere. Certainly nowhere near a restaurant.

Had she been a fool? Had the suggestion of going out to lunch been just a ruse on Luc's part? Perhaps he had brought her here with the intention of making *her* his lunch...?

'Your suppositions are not flattering.' The harshness of his voice cut into her rapidly escalating thoughts. 'Either to yourself or to me!' he added hardly as he turned the car into a deserted car park about half a mile into the forest, before turning to look at her, those finely chiselled features as harsh as his voice. 'If I had asked you out today with the intention of making love to you then, believe me, I would have chosen somewhere more comfortable than a forest floor littered with pine-cones!'

Darci stared at him for several seconds, biting her top lip in an effort to control the smile this image brought to mind. No doubt the intrusion of pine-cones and needles at the wrong moment could play havoc with seduction—even Luc's!

'Better.' Luc grimaced as he saw the laughter gleaming in those moss-green eyes. 'Have a little faith, hmm, Darci?' He sighed before turning to get out of the car and go round and open the boot, giving Darci those few minutes to sit and consider the mistake she had made concerning his intentions.

Not completely, of course.

He did not intend going back to London today without kissing Darci. Maybe a little more than kissing her. But he really would prefer the comfort of a bed when he held her completely naked in his arms and worshipped that beautiful body from the top of her fiery head to the tips of her slender toes.

Of course it wasn't helping his self-control that she looked so stunningly beautiful in a fitted black T-shirt and an above-the-knee-length white skirt that clung to the rounded contours of her bottom. Those long legs were bare and her elegant feet were thrust into cork sandals.

No, there was no way he was going to be able to resist at *least* kissing and caressing Darci today!

When she finally climbed out of the car to join Luc, Darci was no nearer to knowing what they were doing in the middle of a deserted forest than she had been a few minutes ago.

The wicker basket he carried in one hand and the blanket tucked under his other arm gave her the answer she had been looking for....

'A picnic?' Her face lit up. 'Luc, are we going to have a picnic?' she added, as her pleasure grew.

She hadn't been on a picnic in years—not since she was a child with her family, in fact.

But she would never, ever have thought that Luc Gambrelli, mega-rich sophisticated film producer, who probably ate at exclusive restaurants like Garstang's every night of the week, would enjoy eating his meal alfresco....

'You're letting your unflattering thoughts show again, Darci,' he reproved dryly, before turning to look around them. 'Over that way, I think.' He nodded in the direction of a well-worn path.

'Can I carry anything?' she offered, as an apology for what he had guessed were her less than flattering thoughts about him.

'The blanket.' He handed it to her. 'That way we both have a hand free,' he observed with satisfaction, and he reached out with his own free hand to lace his fingers intimately with hers.

Completely throwing Darci's equilibrium off-balance again as she realised that, although this park might be busy at the weekends, with urbanites escaping the city, on a Tuesday lunchtime it was virtually deserted. The only other people around were another couple who had arrived in separate cars as Luc was locking the Porsche, who Darci suspected of a romantic tryst. A suspicion they seemed to confirm when, after one furtive glance around them, they scooted off in the opposite direction to the one Luc and Darci were taking!

'You're making assumptions again, Darci,' Luc said as he strode towards the pathway. 'Probably correct ones this time, though,' he conceded. 'But I make it a point of principle never to pass judgement on other people's actions.'

Because there were so many people willing to pass judgement on *his* actions? Darci wondered as they wended their way through the denseness of the trees.

Including her.

But there was no excuse for the heartless way he had treated Mellie, she told herself stubbornly. The way he would treat her, too, if she gave him the chance!

Well, she wouldn't give him that chance.

Something that might be a little difficult to avoid when the two of them were alone in the middle of deserted forest, miles from anywhere!

Luc's mouth tightened and he decided to ignore the thoughts he could see from Darci's expressive face were churning through her over-active imagination. He gritted his teeth as he continued to stride through the forest to where he could hear the sound of water running, for the first time considering his reputation with women might be a curse rather than an asset.

Maybe it was because of the glitzy, ephemeral world of movie-making that he usually inhabited, but Luc knew he had never met anyone quite like Darci before. The things that attracted other women to him—his undoubted power, his wealth, his reputed prowess in the bedroom—cut absolutely no ice with Darci Wilde. She viewed all of those things with the same suspicion she obviously felt about him, and Luc knew that for every two steps forward he took with Darci he also took one back.

And patience, as he knew, had never been one of his virtues!

'Oh, this is lovely!' Darci turned to him to enthuse warmly as they reached a clearing in the forest with a small stream running through its centre. The flattened grass bordering the stream bank showed evidence of other people having picnicked there recently.

Luc found himself entranced by her obvious pleasure. He saw her green eyes glowing as she moved smilingly to the stream's edge, knowing from her approval that he had chosen well by deciding to bring her on a picnic today, that these surroundings suited her much better than the glitter and falseness to be found in a restaurant like Garstang's.

Making him wonder what had made Darci demand that he take her somewhere so sinfully expensive in the first place?

Except, as he was now utterly convinced, she had never had any intention of turning up for that date.

And he still didn't know the reason why....

'Food,' he announced abruptly. 'As you're aware from Sunday evening, I'm much more amenable when I've been fed!'

Mellower had been the word he'd used, Darci remembered, with a return of her wariness as she moved to spread the blanket beside the stream before going down on her knees to help Luc unpack the picnic basket.

And a mellower Luc Gambrelli in these already relaxing surroundings could prove irresistible!

'Goodness, there's enough food here to feed ten people rather than just two!' she exclaimed, as they laid out pâté, pieces of cooked chicken, prawns, boiled eggs, cheeses and salad, as well as two freshly cooked baguettes, and a cooling carton revealing fresh strawberries and a carton of cream. There was also a bottle of chilled white wine and two cut-glass goblets.

'You can thank the hotel staff at Gambrelli's for that,' Luc replied, as he opened the bottle of wine and poured some of the chilled liquid into the glasses.

Of *course* he would have had the picnic prepared at the hotel where he was staying, Darci acknowledged, with a faint feeling of disappointment, knowing she would have appreciated this treat more if Luc had taken the trouble to prepare the picnic food himself. It certainly would have been less impersonal.

'Now what have I done?' Luc prompted warily.

Darci looked at him from beneath lowered lashes and was struck anew by the way he looked: his hair was a gleaming gold, his eyes a warm indulgent brown, and those aristocratic features were almost too perfect to be true. Steely strength melded with raw sensuality. His body was lean and powerful, exuding that same sensuality even relaxed, as he was now as he sat beside her on the blanket.

The plain, totally honest truth was that this man didn't need to do anything to make her completely aware of him!

'You think I should have gone out this morning and bought the things for the picnic *myself*?' he guessed, sounding slightly miffed at her continued silence.

Darci saw what he meant; the image of Luc Gambrelli wandering around a supermarket delicatessen choosing the meats and cheeses for their picnic wasn't an easy one to envisage!

It was also slightly disconcerting that, in some areas at least, Luc seemed to be able to read her mind.

She only hoped he wasn't as knowledgeable concerning her increasing physical awareness of him…

'You're quite right,' she told him briskly as she straightened. 'It was a totally ridiculous thought.'

What did this woman want from him? Luc fumed inwardly as they helped themselves to the array of food.

He was already behaving completely out of character by pursuing Darci in this relentless way. Especially after her verbal put-downs and the deliberate way she had left him waiting at the table for her at Garstang's for over half an hour, before telephoning the restaurant to let him know she wasn't coming after all.

If any other woman had done something like that to him—

But Darci wasn't just any woman, he realised reluctantly, and, as she had told him repeatedly, neither was she in the least impressed by who or what he was.

She looked like a mermaid, sitting there on the blanket with her legs tucked beneath her and all that beautiful red hair flowing silkily about her shoulders and down over her breasts and spine.

A red-haired siren probably more aptly described her, he corrected himself frowningly—Darci was certainly a lure that he didn't seem able to resist!

'What's Luc short for?'

He blinked, focusing on her question with effort, his eyes narrowing warily as he saw the teasing smile playing about her lips. Lips that were bare of gloss today, and all the more temptingly sensual in their naturally pouting pink state.

Dammit, couldn't he think of anything other than how each individual part of this woman's body attracted him? How the whole nearly drove him to distraction?

'Luciano,' he supplied.

'Oh.' She nodded.

'Why?' he enquired shrewdly, as she continued to repress what he was sure was a smile.

She widened innocent green eyes. 'It had occurred to me that Lucifer seemed more apt, that's all,' she confessed.

The rebel angel.

The fallen angel.

'Oh, lighten up, Luc!' Darci laughed openly as he scowled at the realisation. 'Don't you know when you're being teased?' she chided him lightly.

In truth, the only people who usually dared to tease him were Wolf and Cesare. But that was because one of them was his brother and the other his cousin. It was a complete novelty to have a woman treat him with the same disregard, the same familiarity, that they did.

And, seconds ago, hadn't he been considering Darci as a siren, a woman who lured men to their destruction?

'Ha-ha, very funny,' he said, in a decidedly unamused voice.

She had enjoyed herself, Darci realised half an hour later, as they packed the remains of their food back into the picnic basket.

Luc, after his show of pride at being teased, had set himself

out to be an entertaining luncheon companion, regaling her
with amusing stories and anecdotes about people she had only
ever seen on the big or small screen. Not derisive or hurtful
stories, simply ones that had made her laugh at the ridiculous-
ness of some of the demands of the world those people were
forced to inhabit. That Luc inhabited, too.

'Mmm, this is nice,' Luc groaned with pleasure, as he lay
down on the blanket with his head resting on her bent knees.
'Are you comfortable like this?' He turned to quirk one brow
questioningly.

Comfortable, yes.

Relaxed, no.

How could she possibly relax with the warmth of Luc's head
against her thighs? With all that silky gold hair splayed across
her skirt, making her fingers itch to reach out and touch it?

She wanted to touch all of him, she realised achingly as
her gaze travelled over the wide expanse of his chest, the taut
flatness of his stomach, the leanly muscled power of his thighs
and long legs....

'Darci...?'

She raised heavy lids to look at his face, recognising the
same power in those beautifully chiselled features. His high
cheekbones, his nose, long and straight, his mouth—that eroti-
cally tempting mouth—curved into a sensuous smile.

Luc could feel Darci's tension—see and feel the heat of her
gaze on him. Flames seemed to leap in those green depths as
he turned and moved slowly, inch by inch, up her body, feeling
an increase in her anticipation as her legs straightened and she
fell back against the blanket. Luc took the opportunity to
move completely over her. Her arms came up about his neck
and she pulled his head down and he claimed her lips with

his. Soft, sensual lips. Demanding lips, that claimed, possessed, with the same hunger that coursed through him.

Luc groaned as he surrendered to that hunger....

CHAPTER SEVEN

DARCI was aware of Luc with every responsive part of her—lips, hands, skin—all sensitised to the feel of the hard length of his body as he lay above her. Her fingers revelled in the feel of the muscles rippling across his back as his lips continued to plunder, to claim, his tongue stroking lightly, questioningly, against her lips, taking their parting as his answer before moving silkily inside, where he began to probe and lick and taste her.

She felt the warm silkiness of that tongue claim her—gently, and then more demandingly, as the thrusts of his tongue became rhythmic, dancing, duelling with hers, as her body came alive, aching, heated. Darci groaned low in her throat, knowing she craved the touch of his hands upon her, inside her.

She knew that Luc had heard, understood her need, as one of his hands moved restlessly over her ribcage—close, so close to her aching breasts, and yet still not quite touching. Those fingers moved featherlight against her, like the gentle beat of butterfly wings.

His lips left hers to move with moist open-mouthed kisses down the long column of her throat, evoking a pleasure that went all the way down to her toes.

'Please…!' she pleaded urgently, her back arching with her need. That request turned to a long, shuddering sigh as she felt Luc's hand curve about her breast over her T-shirt. Long fingers circled her with excruciating promise, until she cried out again and the pad of his thumb flicked against that hardened nub, sending rivulets of heat and fire between her thighs as her breasts grew heavy and full.

Luc had felt his control slipping the moment Darci arched against him. Even the thin material of her T-shirt was too much. He wanted to feel flesh against flesh, half achieving it as he pushed her top up to gaze down on the lush fullness of her breasts, her pouting nipples. Those deep rose tips were a temptation he couldn't resist, and he bent his head and took her into his mouth, stroking his tongue across their hard arousal.

He was instantly rewarded by Darci's fingers curling into his muscled shoulders, nails digging into his flesh. Luc welcomed that pleasure-pain as he laved, suckled and tasted, drawing her deeper and deeper into his mouth. He couldn't seem to get enough of her.

She was like fire in his arms, molten lava, and the restless caress of her hands, her lips, threatened to burn them both in flames as Luc's thighs moved demandingly against hers, rubbing against her mound. He knew by the way she stroked against him that he had found her sensitive nub, was feeling himself become moist at that friction of movement. He knew that Darci was wet, too, that those swollen pink lips were weeping for his possession.

And he wanted to take her. Right now. Wanted her with a madness that was wild, almost beyond his control.

That *was* beyond his control!

His caresses became more demanding, more intimate, as

he pushed her skirt up, his hand moving unerringly to the inferno that burned between Darci's thighs.

She came to her senses as she felt the brush of cool air against her bared skin—as she realised that it was happening again!

That maybe she had been wrong after all—and Luc *was* irresistible to all women.

No!

She couldn't do this. Wouldn't do this. Would not become just another woman that Luc Gambrelli—the totally irresistible Luc Gambrelli—had seduced.

She wrenched her mouth from his to glare up at him. 'Don't, Luc!' she told him forcefully.

'Don't...?' he repeated in surprise, his eyes dark and stormy, a flush to those high cheekbones.

'No,' she confirmed determinedly as she straightened her clothing. 'Unless it was a lie when you claimed you didn't intend making love to me on a bed of pine-cones?'

Luc stared down at her for several long, tense moments, before rolling onto his side and then onto his back, his arm up over his eyes as he breathed deeply.

Darci lay on the blanket beside him, staring sightlessly up at the sky, totally disorientated by what had just happened. She had wanted Luc—wanted him with a fierceness that had bordered on mindless madness.

And made a complete nonsense of her avowal that a man like Luc Gambrelli would never succeed in seducing her!

She swallowed hard before moistening passion-swollen lips. 'I don't intend being added to your list of conquests,' she told him disgustedly.

Luc didn't move, his eyes, his dark, expressive eyes, still hidden beneath his upraised arm. 'No?' he breathed harshly.

Darci could hear the heavy rise and fall of his chest, and she moved up on her elbows to look down at him, feeling the friction of her T-shirt against her nipples, which were still hard with recent arousal.

'No,' she assured him, with more firmness than conviction—she had wanted him so badly a few minutes ago that she had completely forgotten who and what he was! 'So you may as well call off the hunt as far as I'm concerned.'

Luc raised his arm to look up at her with narrowed eyes. 'Is that how you feel?' His mouth twisted. 'Hunted?'

She wasn't sure how she felt! Luc brought out a hunger in her, a yearning, aching need that she had never known before. She had no experience to deal with it.

This was Luc Gambrelli—the man she had sworn would never get past her defences, the man she had only spoken to at all on Thursday evening because of Mellie, because she'd wanted to let him know that not every woman was susceptible to his lethal charm.

So much for that claim!

Her face fell. 'I can assure you that I'm in absolutely no danger of falling in love with you!' she told him scathingly.

'That's good—because love doesn't enter into my future plans, either,' he came back mockingly.

Oh, she knew that. She was only too well aware of what his intentions were after the way he had behaved with Mellie. The way he would behave with her, too, if she let him. And she seemed to be giving him every opportunity to do that....

'I meant with a man like you,' Darci came back tartly.

His mouth tightened, his gaze glacial. 'I'm not sure I like your implication,' he rasped.

'Oh, come on, Luc,' Darci retorted. 'Any woman falling in love with you would simply be stupid!'

Love had never entered into any of his plans, Luc admitted—in fact, he had spent a lifetime avoiding the emotion…avoiding that damned Gambrelli Curse.

But no woman had ever dismissed him in this derogatory way before. Darci seemed to have taken delight in doing exactly that several times in the last few days.

He turned on his side, knowing by the way Darci stiffened and moved slightly away from him that she wasn't as immune to his close proximity as she claimed to be.

A hard, humourless smile curved his lips. 'Very stupid,' he agreed. 'But lust is something else entirely,' he elaborated. 'I wouldn't object at all if you were to fall in *lust* with me.'

Her eyes widened angrily. 'I'll just bet that you wouldn't!' she cried, before scrambling to her feet, her face flushed with the same anger as she looked down at him. 'Well, that isn't going to happen, either!'

'No?' Luc challenged softly.

'Most definitely not!' she snapped.

Luc smiled confidently as he got to his feet in a leisurely fashion. 'You're a doctor, Darci—what do you think just now was about if it wasn't lust?'

Darci was afraid to even *think* what it had been about!

And she didn't want to talk about it, either….

'I think it's time we drove back to town,' she told him firmly, and she shook the pine needles off the blanket before folding it up and placing it under her arm.

Only to look up and find that Luc hadn't moved, that his dark gaze was still levelled on her consideringly.

'What?' she exclaimed defensively.

'I was just wondering...'

Yes? What had he been wondering?

'Well?' she persisted angrily, as he made no effort to continue.

He let out a ragged breath. 'Nothing important,' he dismissed, bending down to pick up the picnic basket. 'As you said, it's time for us to leave.' He made a grand sweep with his arm that indicated she should precede him down the pathway.

Leaving Darci uncomfortably aware of his dark eyes on her as she walked ahead of him.

Never again, she decided to herself. She didn't care what leverage Luc used—let him come to the hospital in search of her if that was what he chose to do!—she would not agree to go out with him again. Would never again put herself in the position of being vulnerable to the unprecedented desire this man ignited in her.

Luc Gambrelli, of all men!

And the worst of it was, if she hadn't already known of his complete aversion to any sort of commitment to a relationship—given his media reputation and his ruthless pursuit of Mellie, quickly followed by his disappearance out of her friend's life completely once he had made his conquest—then Darci knew she might just have fallen in love with him herself!

She might be a little in love with him anyway....

She stumbled slightly at that realisation, and immediately felt strong fingers move steadyingly about the top of her arm as Luc reached forward to stop her from falling.

'Don't touch me!' she turned to snap coldly, and she wrenched her arm out of his grasp. Probably bruising herself in the process, but not caring, only knowing that she couldn't bear to have Luc touch her when she was feeling so emotionally vulnerable.

Luc drew in a harsh breath as he teetered on the edge of losing his usual self-control.

All of the Gambrelli men had a temper—a red-hot temper that burned so deeply it became icy and steely—but that cold control often gave the impression that they were without emotion at all.

Darci's show of contempt for him was in serious danger of evoking that extreme reaction.

And Luc would guarantee that she wouldn't like it if it did!

He released her to draw in several more controlling breaths. 'You did not seem to find my touch so abhorrent a few minutes ago—in fact, the opposite!' he reminded her frostily, aware that his English had become stilted—a definite sign that he was in danger of losing his temper!

It was something that he had no choice but to turn in on himself, as he saw the way his deliberate cruelty had made Darci's cheeks pale.

But, dammit, why did she have to keep fighting him, fighting herself, when it had to be as obvious to her as it was to him that minutes ago she had wanted—almost begged him—to make love to her?

Why did Darci keep fighting him, fighting the desire that ignited between them every time they were together?

One possibility had occurred to him a few minutes ago—a possibility that he had dismissed the moment Darci had asked him what he was thinking about. Because there was no way, beautiful as she was, and at the age of twenty-eight, that Darci could possibly still be a virgin.

But if she was, then she was completely unknown territory to him.

Territory he would run a mile to avoid!

'You,' she spat out with feeling, the angry colour returning to her cheeks, 'are not a gentleman!'

Luc gave a wince. 'Thankfully, no,' he acknowledged mockingly. 'As I discovered long ago, gentlemen have a lot less fun than I do!'

Darci frowned at him disgruntledly; he didn't have to sound so proud of the fact!

'You're impossible!' she told him disgustedly, before turning and continuing to walk down the pathway. They were almost back to the car, thank goodness.

'So my long-suffering nanny informed me twenty years ago,' he told her unconcernedly as he fell into step beside her.

Her eyes widened. 'You had a nanny?'

'Of course,' he confirmed. 'It's the way of things in the Gambrelli family.' He looked unconcerned at her questioning look. 'Besides,' he added hardly as he strode forcefully across the car park towards the car, 'my mother and father were too busy, too engrossed with each other, to see to the day-to-day needs of their two wild, uncontrollable sons.'

Darci gave him a glance from beneath lowered lashes, sensing there was a lot more beneath that statement than Luc would be willing to admit—possibly a deep-buried hurt. If his parents had been too engrossed with each other to deal with 'the day-to-day needs of their two wild, uncontrollable sons', had they possibly totally excluded their sons…?

Her own parents had a happy, loving marriage, but it wasn't a relationship that had ever excluded either Grant or Darci. However, that didn't sound the case with Luc's parents.

Perhaps that was a possible explanation for Luc's own lack of emotional commitment?

Darci wasn't a psychiatrist, but she had studied mental

health during her general training to become a doctor, and there surely had to be some reason for Luc's total lack of a permanent commitment to any woman. He was thirty-four years old, for goodness' sake; surely he must have fallen in love at least once during those years?

As she had—or rather hadn't!—during her own twenty-eight years? came her next taunting thought.

Well, okay, perhaps there didn't have to be any reason for Luc's determination not to become emotionally involved other than the same kind of decision she herself had made years ago not to become embroiled in any sort of long-term commitment!

But her decision had never been meant as a lifetime one....

Just accept it, Darci, she told herself; there is no other reason for Luc choosing to remain single all these years other than that he's just having far too good a time being footloose and fancy-free to consider the alternative!

'I thought you wanted to leave, Darci?' Luc said pointedly as he stood beside the open passenger door, waiting for her to get in.

'Sorry.' She grimaced, throwing the blanket into the boot before striding round to slide economically inside the car, not even risking another glance at Luc as he stood looking down at her for several long seconds before moving to get in behind the wheel.

The drive back to London seemed even longer to Darci than the one coming out had been. She was totally aware of Luc's brooding presence beside her as he steered them smoothly and efficiently back to the city.

Enforcing her earlier realisation that today had been yet

another disaster as far as keeping her distance from Luc was concerned. She just couldn't seem to stop herself, to resist, when he took her in his arms!

'I'm coming up with you,' Luc announced arrogantly, once he had parked the car outside her apartment building.

Darci gave him a sharp look. 'Why?'

His mouth twisted. 'Not for the reason you obviously think!' he snapped derisively. 'But I believe it's time—past time!—that you told me what all this has been about,' he stated as he got out of the car.

He had come to a decision on the drive back. A decision he had every intention of carrying through before he and Darci parted today. Probably for the last time…

He knew by the way her gaze suddenly avoided his that he hadn't been mistaken in his conclusions concerning Darci's unpredictable behaviour the last few days. There really was something behind the way she kept blowing hot and then cold—literally!

'I'm not leaving until you tell me the truth, Darci,' he warned her harshly, after opening the passenger door for her to get out.

Which she did reluctantly. 'I have no idea what you're talking about, Luc—'

'Darci, the people who know me well,' he cut in, deceptively mildly, 'would tell you that my present mood is not a good time for you to continue to be economical with the truth.'

'To lie, you mean?' she challenged.

He gave a terse inclination of his head. 'To lie,' he confirmed grimly.

'How dare you?' She turned on him, those green eyes sparkling angrily. 'I—'

'And no amount of feigned anger on your part is going to distract me from getting a truthful answer from you,' Luc assured her softly.

'Feigned?' she repeated furiously, her hands clenched at her sides, those magnificently full breasts surging up and then down as she breathed agitatedly. 'Let me assure you, Luc, that I don't have to pretend to be angry with you. Most of the time that's exactly how I feel!'

He smiled tightly. 'And the rest of the time you are liquid desire in my arms…'

'You bast—'

'No, I don't think so, Darci,' he advised, and he caught her arm as her hand arced up with the obvious intention of slapping his face. 'We are attracting attention,' he warned her. He knew they were the focus of avid glances from the couple in the process of walking past them down the street.

Colour warmed Darci's cheeks as she gave the couple a frowning glance. 'You're the one who's attracting their attention, Luc,' she hissed heatedly. 'Not surprisingly, when you're the great, the legendary Luc Gambrelli—'

'That is enough!' Luc bit back harshly, his fingers tightening painfully about her arm as he clamped her to his side to march her forcefully into her apartment building. 'Don't!' he warned Darci as she would have protested, aware of just how close this woman was to making him lose his temper completely.

Darci didn't. She knew, from the cold waves of anger emanating from Luc as he maintained that hold on her arm to march her up the stairs to her flat, that she had pushed him beyond the limit of his patience—that he was now going to demand some answers from her. And, as he said, they had better be truthful ones.

He had no intention of going anywhere until she gave them to him....

CHAPTER EIGHT

THE man she faced across her sitting-room a few minutes later wasn't Luc Gambrelli the seductive charmer, the man Darci had known up until now, or the businesslike film producer Grant claimed him to be. No, this man was something else entirely. A cold, icy stranger who had no intention of giving her any quarter whatsoever.

Sorry, Mellie. She made a mental apology to her friend, knowing that there was no way she was going to be able to get through this present conversation without bringing the other woman into it. And never had it been truer than at this moment that attack was the best form of defence...

'Mellie Chandler,' she bit out tersely.

Luc continued to look, at her with cold, unblinking eyes, the harshness of his expression unchanging.

'Melanie Chandler.' She impatiently used her friend's full, professional name.

There was still no sign of recognition in Luc's face—not even a raise of that arrogant eyebrow.

'Oh, come on, Luc,' Darci snapped shortly as she threw her handbag down onto one of the armchairs. 'I know it's been a few weeks, but surely you haven't forgotten Mellie already?'

Luc had already gathered by Darci's aggressive repetition of the name Mellie—Melanie Chandler—that it was supposed to mean something to him.

Except that it didn't.

He had never even heard the name before, let alone forgotten the woman!

'What about her?' he prompted guardedly.

Darci eyed him scathingly. 'She's a friend of mine. And Grant's, incidentally,' she added challengingly. 'In fact, she's the absent flatmate I told you about,' she reminded him. 'She's an actress, and currently living in LA,' she added impatiently, as Luc continued to look blank.

Luc frowned. 'And…?'

'And you pursued her until you caught her, took her to your silk-sheeted bed with promises of furthering her acting career and then you dumped her!' Darci accused disgustedly.

To his certain knowledge Luc had never viewed promises of furthering an acting career as a means of seducing any woman into his 'silk-sheeted bed'.

Despite the amount of women who were supposed to have shared that bed, he never forgot the names of the women he had been intimately involved with. He was absolutely certain Melanie Chandler had not been one of them.

Certainly not in the last few weeks. He hadn't been involved with any woman but Darci herself in the three months since Wolf's wedding!

'I did?' Luc looked completely puzzled.

'You know you did!' Darci snapped resentfully.

'Exactly when did I do this?' he prompted softly. 'A few weeks ago, I believe you said…?'

'Oh, for goodness' sake, Luc,' Darci threw at him as she

began to restlessly pace the room. 'Mellie is a very close friend, and I know exactly what happened between the two of you, so you might just as well stop this pretence now.'

Really—did the man think she was totally stupid? Or was he just playing for time, giving himself a chance to come up with an acceptable excuse for the callous way he had treated Mellie? If he was, he was wasting his time!

'When, Darci?' he demanded, in a tone that brooked no argument.

He really was rather intimidating in this mood, Darci acknowledged with an inward grimace. His irresistible charm was completely erased from the face of this coldly determined stranger.

She shook her head. 'You began pursuing her eight weeks ago, showering her with flowers and compliments, promises of getting her a part in the latest film you were producing, and then you dumped her two weeks later, after she had shared your bed!'

Luc's mouth tightened. 'And I did this after "showering her with flowers and compliments, promises of getting her a part in the film I was producing"?' he repeated with a pained wince. 'Let me assure you, Darci, that I have never needed to use such empty promises to persuade a woman into sharing my bed.'

Darci's cheeks flushed as she recalled that he certainly hadn't needed to use those ploys on *her* to have her hot and wanting in his arms. Much to her self-disgust!

'You used them on Mellie,' she accused angrily, that anger directed at herself as much as at Luc; she, too, had almost been persuaded by the novelty of a picnic, for goodness' sake!

'No,' Luc said flatly.

A frown marred Darci's brow. 'What do you mean, no?'

'I mean, no,' he bit out tersely. 'I have never met anyone

called Mellie—or Melanie—Chandler. And as I have never met her, I certainly haven't seduced her into my bed—with or without flowers, compliments and promises of furthering her career!' he finished disgustedly.

He abhorred the men in his profession who did use such enticements on young and beautiful actresses, who were often tricked into believing that going to bed with those men would help their careers—especially as it invariably didn't. It was usually the ones with little talent for acting who resorted to the casting couch, because any actress of any repute would make it on her own merits, without having to reduce herself to that level.

The fact that Darci believed him to have behaved in just that fashion with a close friend of hers certainly explained her odd behaviour the last few days.

It also explained why Darci was so confused about her own response to him....

Because she hadn't expected to be attracted to him, Luc realised grimly. Had thought merely to attract him and then shun him, as recompense for hurting her friend.

All of this—Darci's barbed conversation which had so attracted him when they'd met at the film premiere, the way she had deliberately stood him up at Garstang's two evenings later, the pointedly cutting remarks she had made since—had been to exact revenge on him for using and then discarding her friend Mellie!

A woman he had never even met, let alone seduced into his bed!

Darci stared at Luc, more than a little wary of the evidence of his steadily increasing annoyance in the cold glitter of his eyes and the nerve that pulsed in his tightly clenched jaw.

Something was wrong here—very wrong….

She swallowed hard. 'I don't believe you,' she told him weakly.

'No,' he grated. 'I can see that you don't.'

Her mouth felt very dry. 'Well?' she challenged at his continued silence.

Very, *very* wrong, she acknowledged, and she moved her slightly shaking hands behind her back, so that Luc shouldn't see how nervous his icy stillness was making her.

But Luc's claim never to have even met Mellie couldn't be true, could it?

Of course it couldn't!

If it was, then Mellie was the one who was telling fibs—and what possible reason could her friend have for inventing such a story?

None whatsoever. Which meant that Luc had to be the one who was lying after all.

Or that he had such a succession of women parading through his bed that he really had forgotten Mellie!

Darci let out a sigh. 'Let's just stop all the pretence, Luc—'

'I would be glad to,' he agreed, his eyes glittering with altogether another intent as he began to move stealthily towards her.

'Wh—what are you doing?' Darci prompted nervously, even as she took a step backwards from his direct approach.

'Dispensing with the flowers, compliments and promises to further your career, and getting straight on with the seduction into my bed—or, as this is your apartment, *your* bed,' Luc corrected hardly.

'Don't be ridiculous,' she dismissed breathlessly, taking a step back for every one he took forward. Until—once again!—

she found herself with her back pressed up against the wall and nowhere else to go.

Or hide.

Because the determination in Luc's harshly set expression, in the darkness of his eyes, was enough to make Darci want to turn on her heel and run!

Luc came to a halt mere inches away from Darci as she stood pressed against the wall, his mouth quirking as he looked down at her and saw the apprehension in her expressive green eyes.

She might well look apprehensive—Luc couldn't ever remember feeling this cross in his life before. And it was an emotion that demanded to be assuaged.

He had known he wasn't going to like the explanation for Darci's strange behaviour towards him, but until this moment he'd had no idea just how much he wasn't going to like it.

The whole of their relationship had been based upon Darci's plan to exact revenge for what she considered his callous treatment of her friend. It had become obvious that Darci herself didn't even like him!

She liked it when he touched her, though—and that was what he intended doing right now!

'You can't do this, Luc,' Darci protested, as she saw that intent in his dark eyes.

'But I thought this was exactly what you believed I could and would do, Darci?' he came back tauntingly, and he moved so that his hands rested on the wall either side of her head and his body was moulded against hers from chest to thigh. The heated throb of his hardened thighs told Darci all too clearly of his arousal. An arousal fuelled by anger rather than desire...

'No!' was all she had time to groan before Luc's head bent down and his mouth claimed hers in a kiss that seared.

Punished.

Consumed.

Conquered…

She was caught, captured between the hard wall behind her and the equally hard wall of Luc's body, as his mouth continued to plunder hers, taking it, claiming it for his own. His tongue moved between her parted lips in a hard thrust at the same time as his thighs moved evocatively against hers and melted all resistance.

She wanted this man.

Wanted Luc.

Wanted him with an ache that was almost painful in its intensity.

Luc increased the pressure of his mouth on hers, and he heard Darci's groan of surrender only seconds before she angled her head and began to kiss him back, to take and demand his response. Her arms moved up about his shoulders and her fingers became entangled in the thickness of the hair at his nape.

He was furious with this woman—more furious than he had ever been before in his life.

For deliberately enticing him into asking her out when all the time she was intent only on retribution. For not believing him when he claimed he had no idea what or who she was talking about as she accused him of hurting her friend Mellie.

But none of that seemed to matter now as their kisses deepened, became hungry, a sweet torture—until just kisses weren't enough, and Luc knew he had to touch her, that he wanted to feel Darci's naked flesh in his hands, to kiss and touch every heated inch of her until she was pleading for his possession.

He pushed her T-shirt out of the way, his eyes dark as he looked down at the breasts he had bared, so firm and up-sweeping, their tips already as hard as pebbles. He reached to roll one between his thumb and finger, raising his head to watch as pleasure suffused Darci's face, heavy lids falling down over misty green eyes as she pressed herself closer against his hand in silent invitation.

Luc took up that invitation as he reached down to clasp one of her legs and bring it up about his thigh. He moved in closer to her, his hardness pressing against silk as he began to move against her, knowing from the way Darci melted against him and her increasingly breathless groans that his erection was rubbing at the very heart of her pleasure.

He wanted to release himself, push aside that silk barrier and bury himself inside her. *Deep* inside her. Wanted to bury himself to the hilt before stroking deep and hard. Wanted to bring Darci to her knees as she released herself hotly around him.

Instead his hands moved up to capture both of hers, moving them above her head before grasping them tightly in one of his, leaving his other hand free to capture those invitingly thrusting breasts, kneading, caressing, but not quite touching the turgid nipple as he looked down at Darci's flushed face and feverish eyes.

'Please, Luc!' Darci breathed achingly as she offered herself to him. 'Oh, please…!'

Oh, yes, he would please her. He intended pleasuring Darci until she begged. Intended her to know that no woman had ever gone away from his bed less than satisfied, let alone bent on the type of revenge she had tried to exact on him.

'Tell me what you want, Darci,' he encouraged hardly.

She looked stricken as she shook her head. 'I can't…!'

'Yes, you can,' he assured her softly, his fingertips now like butterfly wings against her breast. 'Tell me, Darci!' he repeated harshly.

'Oh, God, no…!' she protested achingly, even as her thighs moved restlessly against his.

'Tell me.' Luc deliberately swept his thumb across the very tip of her nipple, and watched as the ripples of pleasure washed over and through her.

She released a shuddering breath, her eyes closing. 'Touch me…' she groaned. 'For God's sake, touch me! Take me in your mouth, Luc!' She rubbed her silky thighs encouragingly against his.

'Look at me, Darci,' Luc instructed huskily. 'I want you to watch as I pleasure you.'

Darci raised heavy lids, her gaze caught and held by Luc's as he lowered his head and flicked his tongue moistly across her nipple. Her knees almost buckled at the waves of heated pleasure that coursed through her body.

They did buckle as she watched Luc place his lips over that peak before he drew it full into his mouth and began to suck, and all the time that brown gaze locked with hers, and the hardness of his thighs pressed against her ever-increasing wetness as she burned and ached for his full possession.

She wanted him deep inside her—wanted him to release her from this pleasure that was becoming almost painful as it intensified and swirled over and in her.

She felt hot, so hot, and so achingly wet between her thighs. Her cry was one of longing as Luc's mouth left her and she saw the full, thrust of the nipple he had just suckled to full erection.

'Tell me what else you want, Darci,' he encouraged as his tongue once again rasped moistly against that fullness.

'Touch me again, Luc!' she groaned.

'Where?' He stroked his tongue over her other nipple, setting off more ripples of heated pleasure. 'Tell me, Darci. Show me!' he urged roughly, and he released one of her hands to bring it downwards.

She hesitated only fractionally before taking his hand from her other breast and moving it lower, much lower, placing it against her silkiness, showing him exactly what she wanted. Needed. Hungered for.

Her back arched, her head falling back as Luc touched the very centre of her, the soft pad of his thumb finding that hardened nub. He began to caress her, lightly, rhythmically, before he increased the pressure and fire threatened to ignite and explode.

She thought she *would* explode as Luc's tongue laved across the aching hardness of her nipples, first one and then the other. With the same hypnotic rhythm his hand caressed her, and he entered her with two fingers, those deep thrusts reaching into the very heart of her, touching off waves of sensation that took her to the edge of trembling completion.

'Oh, oh, *oh*…!' Darci cried as Luc's thumb continued to caress and rub her sensitive nub as he took her higher and deeper into the realms of sensual pleasure.

Luc gentled the thrusts of his fingers before removing them completely when he felt Darci's inner tightness start to contract with the ripples of impending release. 'Not yet, Darci,' he murmured huskily as she looked down at him with mute pleading; she hadn't begged nearly enough yet! 'Remember my fantasy of that first evening, Darci?' he reminded her lazily. 'Remember…?' he prompted, and he dropped down onto his knees in front of her.

His gaze held hers as he slipped her silky panties down the lean length of her thighs to throw them to one side and then place one of her legs over his shoulder, completely exposing the moist and swollen pink lips of her full arousal to his gaze…and his mouth.

He laved his tongue over her hardened nub, first strongly and then with gentle sweeps, tasting her as her juices flowed. His tongue was deep inside her now, with strong, hard thrusts that he could once more feel taking her to the edge of sobbing release.

Again he stopped, looking up at her with dark eyes as her hands closed convulsively about his shoulders. Her gaze was feverish as she looked down at him imploringly.

Luc sat back slightly before reaching up to cup the fullness of her breasts, watching Darci's face as his thumbs moved across her nipples in a brief caress. He saw her breath catch in her throat even as a spasm of renewed pleasure coursed through her. Luc knew exactly what she wanted from him as her hands tightened on his shoulders and she drew him towards the dewy warmth of her moistness.

He would only have to touch what was hidden beneath those silky curls with the tip of his tongue now, he realised, just one moist caress and she would disintegrate in front of his eyes as he gave her the release she ached for.

For a moment indecision raced through him—the need to give Darci what she wanted set against the fact that he knew she was only using him, that she didn't even like him.

His face set into harsh lines as he made his decision, surging to his feet to sweep Darci up in his arms.

'What are you doing?' she groaned protestingly.

Luc glanced down at her as he strode forcefully across the

room. 'Taking you to bed,' he rasped. 'That is what you want, isn't it?' Darci looked up at him uncertainly, finding no hint of the tender lover in his harshly set expression and the darkness of his eyes. 'Luc, what—? Luc…!' she cried, as he didn't place her on her bed, but instead dropped her from a three-foot height so that she bounced on the springy mattress.

His mouth twisted derisively as he looked down at her, and she tried to regain her balance enough to straighten her clothing over her exposed body. 'I said I was taking you to bed, Darci—not that I would be joining you there!' he informed her evenly.

Darci swallowed hard, not understanding any of this—not understanding Luc. He had been as aroused as she still was a few minutes ago, hadn't he?

Hadn't he…?

Luc continued to look coldly down at her in a way that said otherwise. 'I suggest that the next time you speak to your friend Mellie you ask her why she lied to you when she told you she and I had been lovers,' he grated hardly.

'What…?' Darci couldn't think straight. Her body was still on fire with the need Luc had lit deep inside her but left unassuaged.

Deliberately?

Had he aroused her on purpose, touched her, caressed her, with the sole intention of humiliating her?

'Oh, I think you understand me perfectly well, Darci,' he said, his gaze once again sweeping over her disdainfully. 'I've never even met your friend Mellie, let alone showered her with flowers, compliments and empty promises in order to seduce her into my silk-sheeted bed,' he stated plainly, so that there should be no lingering misunderstanding.

Darci blinked up at him, trying to make sense of what he was saying. 'But she said— She—'

'I don't give a *damn* what your friend Mellie said, Darci,' Luc informed her disgustedly. 'I have never met the lady— if, indeed, that's what she really is,' he added, with a scathingly dismissive curl of his top lip.

Darci couldn't mistake the utter conviction in his voice for anything other than the truth, and she looked up at him dazedly, could clearly see freezing emotion in the harshness of his expression. She realised fully now what had been behind Luc's seduction minutes ago—his deliberate seduction.

And if what he claimed was indeed the truth, then Darci knew she deserved the contempt she could see blazing down at her in those compelling brown eyes....

But if Luc *was* telling the truth then that meant Mellie had lied. And Darci still couldn't see any reason, any scenario, in which her friend would need to do that.

She gave a shake of her head. 'There's absolutely no reason why Mellie would lie to me—'

'I have no explanation for how or why Melanie Chandler lied to you, Darci,' Luc cut in coldly. 'I only know that she did lie! In the same way that *you* have lied—from the very beginning of our acquaintance to the bitter end,' he added, his meaning more than clear.

Luc was telling her that after today she would never see him again.

'If in the next twenty-four hours you feel the need to check with the Gambrelli Hotel, you will find that I intend staying on in London for several more days on family business,' he continued. 'I am only telling you this because once you have ascertained what really happened from your so-called friend, you may feel the need to apologise to me,' he explained, at her wide-eyed expression. 'I strongly advise you not to give in to the impulse.' His eyes sparked dangerously. 'Because there is nothing that you could have to say to me that I would ever wish to hear!'

With one last disgusted sweep of that hard, uncompromising gaze over her tousled appearance, he turned on his heel and left the room, the apartment door slamming behind him with controlled violence only seconds later.

Darci fell weakly back onto the bed to stare up at the ceiling, all arousal, all desire, having dissipated in the face of Luc's cold fury. Her eyes were burning with unshed tears.

Tears of humiliation as she relived her complete abandon in Luc's arms just now, as he'd caressed and touched her more intimately than she had ever been touched before.

But she knew now that Luc had deliberately aroused her, taken her to the very edge of release time and time again before denying her, and that the motivation behind that deliberation hadn't been his own need or arousal but a punishment for Darci's deliberate actions these last six days.

Because Luc denied ever having met Mellie, let alone being involved with her.

But he couldn't be telling the truth.

Could he…?

CHAPTER NINE

'OKAY, Darci, what's going on?' Mellie demanded down the transatlantic telephone line.

'Going on?' Darci came back lightly.

She had tried calling her friend in Los Angeles several times during the last twenty-four hours, with the intention of asking Mellie about her relationship with Luc. But now that she had actually got through to her friend she didn't quite know what to say.

Not without accusing Mellie of being a liar!

And their friendship had been too long established, was too close, for Darci to feel able to do that....

But neither had she been able to dismiss Luc's claims that he had never even met Mellie, let alone had an affair with her. He had sounded so absolutely adamant that he was telling the truth, had been so furious at her accusations—icily so!—that in the end Darci didn't know which one of them to believe. Mellie or Luc.

Hence her phone calls to Mellie...

'Yes—going on,' Mellie repeated dryly. 'Despite being the one to call *me*, repeatedly and urgently, you've spent the last five minutes chatting about everything and nothing. And

Kerry was decidedly evasive when I spoke to her on Saturday,' she added conclusively.

Dear, sweet, loyal, totally ingenuous Kerry, who couldn't tell a lie even if she tried!

Darci took a deep breath. 'I need to talk to you about Luc Gambrelli,' she said bluntly.

There was a stunned silence on the other end of the line for several long seconds. 'Why...?' Mellie finally queried guardedly.

Why?

Because Darci couldn't get Luc's look of total disgust before he'd left her out of her mind!

Because his cold, deliberate anger at her own behaviour had been too genuine to be anything other than the real thing!

Because, incredibly, she now knew she had fallen in love with him herself....

Actually, she had known it the moment Luc had walked out of the apartment door and she'd been overwhelmed with a deep, sinking sense of loss. And the last twenty-four hours, as she'd wrestled with her conscience over her own actions, while at the same time trying to contact Mellie, had only confirmed those feelings.

She had fallen deeply, irrevocably in love with a man who now felt nothing but contempt for her.

With the stunningly handsome, the sexually arousing, the furiously angry with her, Luc Gambrelli!

'Darci...?' Mellie pressed uncertainly. 'Why all this sudden interest in Luc Gambrelli?'

Darci drew in another deep, controlling breath before speaking. 'He was at the film premiere I attended with Grant last Thursday evening.'

'Yes…?'

That continued hesitancy in Mellie's voice unnerved her. Worried her!

'Did it never occur to you, Mellie, that I might meet him?' Darci came back, just as guardedly.

'You *met* him?' Mellie gasped, dismay added to her tone of uncertainty. 'Did you actually speak to him?' she asked worriedly.

'Yes, I actually spoke to him,' Darci confirmed, knowing Mellie too well after all these years of friendship to be in the least fooled by the way her friend kept answering her questions with questions of her own. 'And I'm sure, knowing me as well as you do, that I thought of what you had told me about your involvement with him! Why did you lie about your affair with him, Mellie? *Why?*' she pleaded emotionally, her hand tightly gripping the telephone receiver as she acknowledged that this was exactly what her friend had done.

That Luc had been the one telling her the truth after all….

Luc stared down at the message on top of the pile he had picked up from Reception on his way through the hotel to his suite.

Would you please meet me at Garstang's at eight o'clock this evening?

There was no signature to the message. But there didn't need to be.

Only Darci could have sent such a request, asking him to meet her at the same restaurant—at the same time—as he had arranged previously.

Luc read the message a second time as he stepped into the

lift, torn between crushing the piece of paper to a pulp in his hand and a grudging feeling of admiration for the position Darci had deliberately put herself in.

Because she now knew he had been telling her the truth about her friend Mellie…?

That might be so, but nevertheless Darci had to know that by asking him to meet her at Garstang's, of all places, she was leaving herself open to the same humiliation she had deliberately inflicted on him previously—that he might now be the one not to turn up for the date and leave her sitting at the table, squirming under the curious stares of the other diners.

Luc's anger towards Darci hadn't abated much during the last couple of days, while he'd visited Wolf and then Cesare at their individual family homes outside London, to reassure them that, despite the delay, he would be in Paris by the weekend, as planned.

Those visits had unfortunately also subjected Luc firsthand to his brother's and his cousin's marital happiness!

He had seen as little as possible of his brother and his cousin and their respective spouses these last three months. Not because he didn't like the women Wolf and Cesare had married, but because he did.

His whole family now seemed bent on Luc being the next and the last of the Gambrellis to get married, to the extent that it seemed whenever he visited any of his family, there was always a couple of single women—highly marriageable women—included in the lunch or dinner party. His mother was the worst culprit, constantly presenting eligible heiresses for him to vet as wife material whenever he visited her at the Paris apartment where she had chosen to live after the death of their father.

But Luc only had to see Wolf and Cesare so much in love, so totally besotted with their respective wives, to reassure himself that marriage wasn't for him.

He didn't need to get married; Wolf had inherited the title of Count, and Angel was expecting their first child—the heir—in a few months' time.

Besides which, Luc liked his life exactly the way it was. At the moment he was free to do exactly what he wanted, when he wanted, and the idea of giving up that freedom, of giving his whole heart into someone else's keeping in the way that Wolf and Cesare had, sent a chill down his spine.

None of which answered the question as to whether or not he should meet Darci at Garstang's this evening....

He really shouldn't go—should leave Darci to her humiliation as a sign of his absolute contempt for the things she had believed of him, for the way she had behaved towards him....

Darci had never felt so nervous in her entire life as she did sitting at the table in the middle of the restaurant at eight o'clock that evening. As she waited to see if Luc would actually put in an appearance, or if his disgust with her ran so deeply he wasn't even prepared to meet her here in order to let her apologise.

The restaurant was just as exclusive as she had thought it would be. The *maître d'*, obviously not recognising her as one of the select clientele who usually dined here, had looked down his haughty nose at her as he'd shown her to the table. Compared with her own simple white dress and lack of jewellery, the other diners were all glamorously dressed and bejewelled—although they nevertheless spared her the odd curious glance as they chatted loudly together.

The only consolation Darci had as she sat down to wait was that each table was given a certain amount of privacy by the select placement of potted plants and partitions, allowing her a brief respite from the curiosity of other customers if she wanted it for a few seconds.

What Darci really wanted was not to be here at all!

Not an option, Darci, she told herself firmly, even as she outstared a man seated across the restaurant as speculation showed in his admiring blue gaze. To make matters more embarrassing, Darci was sure she recognized him as a popular actor from a top television programme that she watched whenever she wasn't working!

She looked down uncomfortably at the gleaming glassware and pristine white linen on the table, sure, after sitting here for ten minutes, that Luc wasn't coming.

Not that she altogether blamed him for exacting such retribution. In fact, she had deliberately chosen to meet him at Garstang's so that he could do exactly that if he wanted to. It was the least she owed Luc after the way she had misjudged him.

'Thanks, James. Bring a bottle of Gevrey Chambertin, hmm?'

Luc.

After spending the last ten minutes glancing anxiously towards the door, she had finally missed him when he did arrive!

She looked up at him dazedly as he stood beside the table, bedazzled and slightly breathless at how gorgeous he looked in a dark evening suit and snowy white shirt.

'I'm sorry to be late, Darci. The traffic was heavier than I expected,' he murmured huskily as he slid smoothly into the seat opposite hers.

She didn't care if the London traffic was at a standstill so long as Luc was here, after all!

He looked good. His deep, burnished gold hair gleamed silkily in the muted overhead lighting, his face was all hard, aristocratic angles that reminded her he was the son and brother of a count, and the leashed power of his body was barely restrained by his sophisticated clothes.

But her heart sank as she looked up into a gaze hard with cool impersonality, telling her that Luc might have taken pity on her and come here this evening after all, but that he certainly hadn't forgiven her!

She swallowed hard. 'It's very good of you to have agreed to meet me like this—'

'I have agreed to nothing, Darci,' he cut in icily, his eyes narrowed to slits. 'To have left you sitting alone here would only confirm me as the callous bastard you already consider me to be,' he explained harshly.

Would reduce him to the same level that Darci had lowered herself to when she'd deliberately stood him up....

She moistened dry lips. 'Luc, I owe you an apology—'

'Thank you, Paul.' He turned to smile warmly at the wine waiter as he arrived beside the table with a bottle of red wine, and the next few minutes were taken up with uncorking and tasting the vintage.

Giving Darci a few minutes' respite to look at Luc unobserved.

Yes, he was still as nerve-tinglingly handsome as she remembered.

Yes, he still made her feel weak at the knees just to look at him; he completely took her breath away, in fact.

But there was a remoteness about Luc this evening that hadn't been there before. A bleakness that was more than surface deep and that totally eradicated the wicked glint of humour in his eyes which had so surprised her when she'd first met him. It sent shivers of apprehension down her spine!

The fact that she knew she deserved to feel those shivers didn't make them any less effective.

Luc took his time sampling the wine, giving himself a necessary few moments' respite to adjust to seeing Darci again. To recognise that she was even more beautiful than he remembered…!

In fact, he had felt a moment's pure violence when he'd entered the restaurant a few minutes ago and seen her out-staring the avid gaze of a man seated at a table across the room. His own hands had clenched at his sides as he'd resisted the impulse to go to the other man's table and tell him precisely what he could do with his admiring glances.

Not that he could exactly blame the guy for his interest when Darci was looking so absolutely beautiful, in a pure white dress that showed off the tan of her bare arms and throat, no jewellery to detract from her cream skin, and with her lush red hair secured at the sides of her head with two antique silver combs, completely exposing the delicate lines of her face, those moss-green eyes and the pouting mouth which was enough to entrance any man.

'It's fine.' He finally nodded tersely for Paul to pour the wine, waiting until the waiter had left before looking across at Darci with mocking eyes. 'What shall we drink to, Darci?' he taunted. 'New beginnings…?' he ventured sardonically as he lifted his glass for a toast.

Darci found herself swallowing hard a second time since Luc's arrival, not quite knowing how to deal with him in this intimidating mood.

Perhaps she shouldn't have chosen to meet him in a restaurant at all—because all she wanted to do at this moment was apologise and then get as far away as possible from the mockingly scornful man Luc had become!

Her fingers shook slightly as she lifted her own wineglass. 'To an apology given and accepted. I think that might be more appropriate…?' she suggested as she looked at him from beneath lowered lashes.

Luc returned her gaze wordlessly for several long, tension-filled seconds. 'But premature, surely?' he bit out.

Because she hadn't yet apologised?

Or because Luc had no intention of accepting her apology?

But if that was the case, then why was he here?

To punish her, possibly.

And she deserved to be punished after setting herself up as his judge and jury—and then having the audacity to pass sentence on him, too!

But he, in his turn, had passed sentence on her….

She frowned across at him. 'You know, your behaviour the last time we met wasn't exactly gentlemanly,' she reminded him hotly. 'And don't raise that arrogant eyebrow at me,' she warned, as he did exactly that.

He looked surprised. 'Which arrogant eyebrow?'

'Your arrogant *right* eyebrow,' she swung back impatiently, and she glared at that brow, her cheeks burning hotly just from mentioning what had happened between them before he'd left her so ignominiously.

Luc wasn't sure whether to remain angry with Darci or to give in to the impulse he had to laugh as she displayed all the outraged indignation of a bantam hen just at the mention of what had occurred last time they'd met. But he was far from forgiving her yet for her assumptions about him, and definitely didn't want to put things between them back on the same footing as they had been before—and any crack in his mocking line of defence was sure to do that.

He raised his arrogant right eyebrow even further as he looked across at her unemotionally. 'You deserved what happened, you little hypocrite,' he said evenly.

The colour in Darci's cheeks flamed even brighter. 'Perhaps I should just grovel and leave?' she muttered between clenched teeth, and she reached down to pick up her bag.

'I promise that I will give you reason to regret it if you should decide to leave me sitting alone here for a second time!' Luc assured her uncompromisingly.

Darci straightened to look across at him uncertainly, knowing from the rigidness of his set jaw, the hard glitter of his eyes, that Luc wasn't making an idle threat—that he was more than capable of causing a scene if she should decide to get up and leave.

But it was more than a little embarrassing to sit here knowing that he was completely aware of how aroused she had been that afternoon. His accusation that she was a hypocrite told her plainly that Luc knew exactly how close she had been to complete capitulation. That it was only Luc's anger and contempt that had prevented the two of them from making love.

She breathed deeply. 'I can't believe that you really want to have dinner with me....'

His mouth twisted derisively. 'Fishing for compliments, Darci?'

'Not at all,' she assured him hotly. 'It's pretty obvious that you don't really want to be here.'

Luc relaxed back in his seat as he looked at her through narrowed lids. 'If that were the case, Darci, then believe me,

I wouldn't be here,' he replied. 'Although I am curious, knowing how difficult it is, as to how you actually managed to book a table here this evening....'

Darci gave a rueful smile. 'What's the point in having a famous film director as a twin brother if you can't use his name occasionally? I was pretty sure there wouldn't be any fuss made about my slight variation on the truth once you arrived,' she added with a grin.

'*If* I arrived,' Luc reminded her coolly.

She nodded. 'If you arrived.'

'And if I hadn't done so?' he taunted.

Darci shrugged. 'Then I would probably have found myself thrown out into the street by eight-thirty!'

Luc found himself smiling in spite of himself—both at Darci's ingenuity in securing the dinner table and her complete lack of illusion about it. 'Does Grant know you used his name in this shameless way?'

'Of course not,' she answered brightly. 'I love my brother dearly, and the two of us are very close. But I would prefer that even he doesn't know what a complete idiot I've made of myself where you're concerned.'

'A complete idiot, Darci?' Luc questioned.

Yes, a complete idiot, Darci repeated to herself, as she acknowledged that she really was in love with Luc, that she loved him so much that under difference circumstances she would probably have been willing to settle for the affair he had once implied he was more than willing to have with her.

Once. Because it was more than obvious that Luc now felt nothing more than contempt for her. That he had only come here this evening to listen to her apology and so witness her humiliation firsthand.

A fine mess she had made of things where Luc Gambrelli was concerned, she accepted heavily.

She grimaced. 'I really do have to apologise to you, Luc, for the things I said and did to you earlier this week—'

'Do you think we could leave your self-flagellation until *after* we have ordered our food, Darci…?' Luc drawled in a bored voice as he picked up his menu. 'The least you owe me is a sinfully expensive meal, don't you think?' he added, unabashedly reminding Darci of her own words the evening they'd first met.

The *least* she owed him?

Darci picked up her own menu as she stared at Luc warily.

That statement seemed to imply that he had some other form of retribution in mind, too….

CHAPTER TEN

'So,' Luc drawled once the waiter had left with their order. 'What did your friend Mellie have to say about me?'

The moment of truth had arrived, Darci acknowledged heavily to herself as she replaced her wineglass carefully on the table after taking a sip. 'Well, as I'm sure you've obviously deduced, she admitted that the two of you have never even met each other.'

Luc gave a small inclination of his head. 'I had already told you that. But of course you didn't believe me,' he reminded her after giving her a searching look.

'Try to see this from my point of view, Luc.' Darci looked across at him appealingly. 'I've known Mellie over half my life. Of *course* I believed she was the one telling the truth!'

'Of course,' he agreed tersely.

He really was every inch the son of an Italian nobleman at this moment, Darci recognised uneasily. His usual easy-going flirtatiousness and the wicked glint in his eye were no longer in evidence at all. 'Obviously I now know that she wasn't—'

'Obviously,' Luc derided bitingly.

This was so much worse than she had imagined it would

be, Darci realised, and she picked up her glass and took another fortifying sip of the red wine.

But what had she imagined? That she could make her apology and give her explanation, and then the two of them would laugh it off and go on from there?

Luc didn't look as if he found any of this in the least funny!

Neither would she when she got the bill at the end of the evening; she would probably end up in the kitchen doing the washing up for a week to pay it off!

'You find this situation amusing, Darci?' Luc accused as he saw her smile.

She straightened, realising that her thoughts were starting to wander. Hysterically? Probably. She was in love with a man she had insulted to such a degree that he had become a cold, angry stranger.

'No, of course not.' She sighed. 'It's all rather sad, really,' she said. 'You see, Mellie told me all those things about an involvement with you in the hope of making someone else jealous.'

Luc's eyes widened at this explanation. 'Your friend Mellie has—feelings for you?' Not that he particularly cared about a person's sexual inclination—live and let live had always been his doctrine—but he somehow found it slightly distasteful that another woman should want Darci in the way that *he* had wanted her.

Still wanted her.

There was no denying that he did still want her, that the slightest movement of her sensually alluring body and the faintest waft of her perfume were enough to fire his arousal. But it was an arousal he was determined to keep under control!

'Of course not,' Darci answered him disgustedly. 'I wasn't the person Mellie was trying to make jealous!'

Luc gave a puzzled shake of his head. 'Then who was this mysterious person?'

She sighed. 'Grant.'

Luc's eyes widened again. 'Your friend Mellie is in love with your twin brother?'

'So it would appear,' Darci confirmed. 'Apparently she's been secretly in love with Grant for years, but had given up all hope of him ever returning the feeling. In fact, she was involved with someone else until she went to Los Angeles six months ago. But she and Grant met up again there, and the two of them went out for dinner a few times. She began to have hope that perhaps Grant did more than like her after all.'

'Only to discover that he didn't?' Luc deduced.

'Not exactly,' Darci continued. 'From the sound of it the two of them did become—quite close,' she admitted. 'But then Grant went off on location for a couple of months, and didn't so much as call her, and so—so—well—'

'So Mellie decided to try and give him a push in the right direction by letting him know, through you, that she was being hotly pursued by someone else?' Luc suggested wearily.

It sounded extremely contrived when actually put into words, Darci accepted.

Something she had told her long-time friend at great length yesterday evening, once she'd learned the truth.

In fact, she had been absolutely furious with Mellie for the deception. Not least because it meant she now had to apologise to Luc...

'Except you didn't tell Grant, did you?' Luc guessed knowingly, feeling sorry for the lovelorn Mellie even though, at the same time, he could cheerfully have strangled her for creating this totally unacceptable situation between Darci and himself.

Making him wonder what relationship he and Darci might have had without her preconceived prejudice towards him....

Darci shook her head sadly, her glorious hair gleaming with streaks of red and cinnamon in the overhead lighting. 'It never even occurred to me to do so. I only talked to you about it because I thought you already knew! Under normal circumstances I would never betray any of my friends' confidences.'

No, of course she wouldn't. Her defence of Mellie Chandler for what she had perceived as Luc's callous treatment of her friend showed Darci to be a true and faithful friend.

As she would be a true and faithful lover...?

Probably. But Luc didn't *want* a true and faithful lover—or anything else!—in his life.

Luckily Luc was saved from having to make any reply by the arrival of their first course—smoked salmon for Darci and calamari for him.

'So what happens to your friend now?' he prompted several minutes later. 'Is she going to confront Grant with her feelings, or simply walk away, sadder but wiser?'

Darci was pretty sure the cynical Luc didn't have any interest in what happened between Mellie and Grant. Although, considering they were the reason she and Luc had met, perhaps Luc did have a right to know what happened next.

She grimaced. 'She's going to confront him, of course.'

'Of course,' Luc accepted wryly. 'She sounds like a very determined woman to me.' Darci gave him a questioning look. 'Exactly the sort of woman I make a point of avoiding,' he explained.

Was Luc giving *her* a warning not to even think about trying the same sort of tack with him?

Had he guessed—did he know—how Darci felt about him?

Did he think that her invitation to dinner this evening was her own way of behaving like a determined woman out to catch herself a reluctant man?

It would be just too humiliating if he did think those things!

'Don't worry, Luc,' she assured him. 'As I've already told you, any woman who makes the mistake of falling in love with you deserves what she gets!'

He didn't even attempt to contradict her claim as he gave an acknowledging inclination of his head, his mouth a thin, uncompromising line. 'Do you think there will be a happy ending for your brother and Mellie?'

'Maybe,' Darci answered slowly. 'Grant was a little— cagey last week, when I asked him if he had seen Mellie while he was in Los Angeles. I hope so,' she added. 'Despite what you might think after what's happened, Mellie really is a lovely person. And now that I've got over being annoyed with her, I believe she and Grant would be perfect for each other. She really is sorry for involving you in this,' Darci finished, giving up on trying to eat her smoked salmon. The conversation—and the company!—had completely robbed her of her appetite.

'And you?' Luc pushed. 'Are you also sorry?'

'More than you can imagine,' she confirmed. More than she ever wanted Luc to guess or know!

He might not have been involved with Mellie—might never have even met her!—but that didn't change the fact that Luc really was a man who shunned all emotional involvement. It would be too awful if he were to guess how Darci really felt about him.

Luc looked across at her with assessing eyes. 'How sorry are you, Darci?' he pressed.

Darci gave him a sharp look, but she was unable to read anything from his closed expression and those hard, merciless eyes.

Merciless…?

Yes, she had to say that was exactly how Luc's eyes looked at this moment….

Luc's mouth tightened as he saw the sudden wariness in Darci's expression. 'I wouldn't expect any woman to be *that* sorry, Darci!' he told her, with hard impatience at what she had obviously been thinking.

She had the grace to blush. 'In that case, I'm sorry enough to buy you dinner at a sinfully expensive restaurant,' she came back challengingly.

He grimaced. 'Don't be ridiculous, Darci. I'm going to pay for dinner.'

'But—'

'No arguments, Darci.' He silenced her protests, the tone of his voice stern. 'I never intended for you to pay the bill.'

Darci was a not-long qualified, very underpaid doctor, for goodness' sake; of course Luc didn't seriously expect her to buy him a dinner that would probably cost her a week's wages!

'But I do appreciate the offer,' he added, as he easily saw that Darci's feathers were still ruffled.

She drew in a deep breath. 'In that case, I'm very, very sorry for the way I behaved towards you earlier this week.'

His mouth quirked humourlessly. 'Even if you do think my own behaviour when we last met was reprehensible?'

She would never know—he would never *allow* her to know!—how close he had come, how nearly he had thrown all caution to the wind and taken what she had so blatantly offered that day.

But he had known even then that Darci wasn't the sort of woman to have a meaningless affair. And that was all any of Luc's relationships had been. What they would always be.

Let Wolf and Cesare suffer their totally besotted love for their wives. As his father had with his mother. And his Uncle Carlo with his wife. And their grandfather before them. Let them all be the ones to suffer that damned Gambrelli Curse. Luc intended remaining exactly as he was—single and heartache-free!

But just because he didn't intend letting himself become emotionally involved with Darci that didn't mean he couldn't salvage something from this situation….

'I don't *think* your behaviour was reprehensible at all, Luc,' she shot back at him reprovingly. 'We both damn well *know* that it was!'

He shrugged unconcernedly. 'You deserved exactly what you got.'

'That's hardly the point—'

'The point is, Darci,' he cut in menacingly, leaning across the table to add more weight to his words, 'I may not be willing to let you buy me dinner, but you *do* owe me.'

She gave him a startled look. 'Owe you…?' she echoed warily.

He smiled derisively. 'Do you think it possible to take your thoughts out of the bedroom for a few minutes…?' he mocked.

Darci felt colour burning her cheeks. But what else was she supposed to think when Luc came out with phrases like she *owed* him?

He was rich as Croesus, as handsome as Apollo and one of the most successful film producers in the world. If she did indeed owe Luc, then what did she have to give him but herself…?

'Go on,' she invited guardedly.

'I have to be in Paris this weekend—'

'I am *not* going to Paris with you for the weekend!' Darci protested indignantly.

He scowled across at her. 'It's usual to wait until you're asked!'

'Yes. Well. Why mention it if—if you didn't intend asking me to go with you?' she finished determinedly.

Although the mere thought of Luc inviting her to go to Paris with him for the weekend made her go weak at the knees!

She had visited the city once on a school trip, when she was fifteen, and even at that tender age she had recognised it as one of the most romantic cities in the world. Luc Gambrelli and Paris could be an irresistible combination!

'Why, indeed?' Luc conceded dryly. 'You're right. I was going to invite you to accompany me—'

'No!' she told him adamantly. 'No, no, *no*!'

He raised that arrogant eyebrow again. 'One refusal would have been sufficient, Darci,' he observed.

She met his gaze unflinchingly. 'No,' she told him firmly.

'But you haven't heard the full invitation yet, Darci,' he taunted.

'I don't need to.' Her cheeks were flushed, her eyes sparkling deeply green. 'There is no way I would ever agree to accompany you to Paris—or indeed anywhere else—for the weekend.'

'Little prude,' Luc drawled. 'What if I were to promise you that the invitation does *not* include us sharing a bed, that my intentions are not in the least dishonourable?'

'It isn't a question of that…'

'Isn't it?' he queried softly.

No, it really wasn't. The truth was, no matter what Luc's intentions—honourable or otherwise—it was herself she didn't dare trust if she went to Paris with him at the weekend. Not when she was already in love with him....

'Why do you want me to accompany you to Paris?' she probed cautiously.

He sat back, regarding her with cool consideration. 'I have a party to attend, and I would like you to go with me as my partner for the evening,' he finally murmured slowly.

'And you're telling me that you can't find someone else to go with you?' she scoffed disbelievingly. 'Someone who actually *wants* to be with you?' she added pointedly.

She had courage, this little firebrand, Luc acknowledged admiringly, even as he considered her barb about taking a partner who felt positively towards him.

He was sure that most women in Darci's position, having initially so wrong-footed themselves, would have been only too happy to make restitution for the mistake they had made. But not Darci.

He leant further back in his chair as their used plates were removed. 'I have my own reasons for wanting it to be you who accompanies me,' he told her levelly once they were alone again.

'And those reasons are…?'

'Entirely my own,' he told her firmly. 'But I can assure you they have absolutely nothing to do with a bedroom—either yours or mine!' He paused as he could see he had failed to convince her. 'Didn't our last encounter prove to you that I don't lose all control at the sight and touch of your delectable body?' he whipped out harshly, angry all over again as her cheeks paled. With himself this time. For deliberately hurting her.

But what else was he to do when even now he knew he wanted to sweep all the glasses and cutlery from the table, lay

Darci across its pristine white-clothed surface and bury himself deep inside her moist and welcoming body?

Maybe he would be courting unnecessary danger in taking Darci to Paris with him? The desire he felt whenever he was in her company would make it extremely difficult to keep to his promise not to share a bed with her.

But his visits to Cesare's and Wolf's homes during the last two days, and the pointed comments of their wives, Angel and Robin, about the eligibility of the guests—the female guests!—who were invited to his mother's party on Saturday evening, had confirmed that his family, and his mother in particular, were still intent on finding him a bride of his own.

After receiving Darci's invitation to dinner this evening Luc had realised that he might have found a way of avoiding that matchmaking—at least as far as the party on Saturday evening was concerned....

He would take his own partner for the evening. A woman he could parade in front of his family, but one who knew better than to expect anything from him at the end of it!

Darci frowned across the table at Luc, wishing she could read something in his face, but only seeing herself reflected back in those enigmatic brown eyes as he kept his expression deliberately bland, easily meeting her probing gaze.

'Don't look so worried, Darci,' he assured her dryly. 'I'm really not suggesting a clandestine weekend away together!'

'I never suggested that you were,' she came back irritably.

'No?' he countered, that dark brow rising mockingly.

'No,' she came back firmly, under no illusions whatsoever, after his coolness to her this evening, that Luc still desired her.

But she did want to know what he was up to. Why he needed a woman to accompany him to a party in Paris this weekend.

Unfortunately only Luc could tell her that—and another glance at his closed expression told her that he had no intention of doing so.

She shook her head. 'I'm not sure I can get the weekend off—'

'Even someone as dedicated to their job as you must be allowed to take holidays, Darci,' he pointed out.

Well, of course she was allowed holiday time. And she probably could get a couple of days if she asked one of her colleagues to cover for her. But she still wasn't sure she wanted to go to Paris with Luc.

Be honest, Darci, she reproved herself, you really don't trust yourself to go to Paris with Luc!

'I will, of course, pay all your expenses.' Luc cut in on her tortuous thoughts. 'All you have to do is look beautiful and say little.'

'Like all your other women?' she retorted sharply.

'Exactly like all my other women,' he accepted.

She looked at him searchingly. What was he up to? Whatever it was, Luc's guarded features told her he wasn't about to share it with her, she accepted heavily.

'I'll need to think about it,' she told him woodenly.

'Think about it all you like. But I will expect your answer by the end of this evening.'

Her eyes widened indignantly. 'That's hardly *fair*, Luc—'

'I don't recall your actions towards me so far as being fair,' he reminded her.

Luc had a point. More than a point, when Darci recalled how almost her every word and move had until now been motivated by feelings of vengeance towards him.

'Come on, Darci,' Luc cajoled, as he could see that she was

weakening. 'Most women would be only too thrilled at the idea of an expenses-paid weekend in Paris,' he tempted.

'I'm not "most women"!' Darci assured him snippily.

Luc was already well aware of that.

Darci's obvious integrity, and the fact that she was different from any other woman he had been involved with—a doctor, and so obviously not connected with the movie and acting world he inhabited—were actually obstacles, he realised.

But on the positive side was the fact that Darci, unlike any other woman he could have invited, while acting as a shield against his family's matchmaking machinations, also knew without a doubt that there was absolutely no substance to their relationship....

CHAPTER ELEVEN

'I SUPPOSE I should have realised we would be staying in a Gambrelli Hotel,' Darci murmured ruefully once they were installed in the lift, with a porter carrying their bags, travelling up to the suite they would be occupying during this weekend in Paris.

Luc had been withdrawn and uncommunicative on the private jet which had flown them here, sitting in one of the six comfortable armchairs that had occupied the spacious cabin, a pair of rimless glasses perched on the end of his aristocratic nose as he went through some papers he had taken from his briefcase and laid out on the table in front of him.

Leaving Darci completely alone with her thoughts. Which had been extremely tumultuous, to say the least.

Being ushered onto the private jet, where her every need had been seen to by the male steward, had given her a glimpse into the world that Luc usually inhabited. A world that, despite her brother Grant's rapidly increasing luxurious lifestyle, was still completely alien to her.

The deference that had been shown Luc when they'd arrived at the hotel, as a member of the family that owned the Gambrelli chain, had been a little overwhelming, too.

Luc looked up from the pile of messages that had been waiting for him on his arrival at the hotel, his frown lessening slightly as he saw the slight bewilderment in Darci's expressive face. 'It's just a hotel, Darci,' he dismissed easily.

'To you, maybe,' she replied tentatively, as the porter opened the door for them and ushered them inside the suite.

Luc dealt with the porter, before closing the door softly behind the other man as he left, and then strolled further into the suite to join Darci in the sitting-room.

Despite being familiar with the chain owned by his cousin, to Luc this hotel was just like every other top establishment he had ever stayed in in the world: very luxurious, but extremely impersonal.

Although not quite as impersonal as usual, with Darci standing there, her flaming red hair cascading loosely over her shoulders and down the long length of her spine, dressed in tight-fitting denims and a white T-shirt that showed off the lean length of her thighs and legs and emphasised the firm thrust of her breasts!

'I think I would like to take a shower and freshen up,' she announced. 'What time are we leaving for the party?'

'We aren't leaving the hotel, Darci,' Luc answered. 'The party is taking place in one of the reception rooms downstairs,' he elaborated at her bewildered look.

He had deliberately remained aloof from Darci after collecting her from her apartment and during the drive to the airport and their flight. But that didn't mean that he hadn't been completely aware of her the whole time they had been together in the back of the car and then on the plane.

Too aware of her for comfort, he acknowledged.

'My brother, Wolf, and his wife will be joining us here for

drinks at seven o'clock, before we all go downstairs at seven-forty-five to join Cesare and Robin,' he added casually.

Darci's eyes widened at this piece of news. Luc's brother and his cousin and their wives were going to be at the party, too?

Maybe the black dress she had brought with her—the sexily vampish one she had modelled for Kerry last week—wasn't the right choice for this evening, after all?

She had thought—assumed—that the guest list for the party this evening would be mainly actors and actresses, and had chosen her dress accordingly.

'What sort of party is this, Luc?' she prompted.

'My mother moved to Paris after the death of my father more than ten years ago. Every year since, she has hosted her own birthday party—'

'This is your *mother's* party?' Darci echoed disbelievingly. The sexy black dress definitely hadn't been the right choice!

Thank goodness she had included a black silk wrap, in case the evening was cool and they had some distance to travel to the occasion.

But this evening was a birthday party for Luc's mother....

'What's this all about, Luc?' she demanded. 'And please don't fob me off by telling me that it's all in my own head,' she warned, as he would have spoken. 'I think, now that we're actually here, I have a right to know what's going on.'

Luc looked at her consideringly, weighing up the pros and cons of taking Darci into his confidence.

On the one hand she didn't need to know his reasons for bringing her here.

But on the other Darci would probably be able to play her part as a buffer between him and the women he knew, from talking to Angel and Robin, his mother had deliberately invited for him to meet tonight more convincingly if she *did* know the truth.

He sighed. 'Both Wolf and Cesare have married in the last year.'

Darci eyed him warily. 'Yes…?'

Luc hesitated. 'The general consensus of my family seems to be that it's time I joined their ranks,' he admitted reluctantly.

Darci continued to look at him consideringly for several long seconds, and then a look of unholy glee entered those beautiful moss-green eyes. 'You have a matchmaking mama!' she exclaimed laughingly.

Luc gave her a look of intense irritation at such blatant humour at his expense. 'Yes, I do.' He grimaced. 'And, whilst I wish I could share your humour on the subject, I most assuredly don't! My family, and especially my mother, have presented a number of likely candidates for the role of my future wife during the last three months—to the point where I have avoided even having dinner with a woman during that time!'

Except with her, Darci realised. But perhaps she didn't count?

'Which was how you were so sure you and Mellie hadn't been involved,' she deduced.

'Exactly!' His grim expression deepened as he moved to the fridge and took out a half-bottle of champagne. 'Would you like some?' he offered, as he poured the bubbly wine into a glass.

Darci had no idea why she had been laughing minutes ago. Luc's aversion to marriage was obviously so strong he was even willing to use emotional blackmail over her vengeance towards him in order to have her accompany him to his mother's birthday party and act as a beard!

Because he clearly considered her to be absolutely no threat to his emotions or his bachelor state!

'Why not?' She accepted the glass of bubbling champagne, taking a much-needed sip. 'I wish you had explained the situation before bringing me here, Luc. I'm really not happy about deceiving your family in this way,' she explained, as he looked at her questioningly.

He shrugged unconcernedly. 'All you have to do is cling to my arm all evening and look beautiful—which you undoubtedly are—and smile and say little. What's the problem?'

The problem was he wanted a woman on his arm this evening he knew wasn't in love with him.

And Darci was very *much* in love with him—was becoming more so by the minute!

Besides, she really didn't like the idea of practising such a deception on his family. Especially if that family turned out to be more perceptive concerning Darci's feelings for Luc than he was. If that should be the case, then this whole charade might just completely backfire in Luc's arrogantly handsome face!

'I don't like it, Luc,' she told him frankly. 'I would never have agreed to coming here if I had known you intended deceiving your family in this way.'

Luc had realised that. He had come to know Darci much better during the last week than she gave him credit for. But with his mother's birthday party looming nearer every day, he had known he had to take some sort of step to prevent his family's unwanted interference in his personal life. Unfortunately for Darci the situation between the two of them had presented the ideal opportunity for him to do just that.

'It's just one evening of your life, Darci,' he dismissed unconcernedly. 'And then the two of us won't ever need to see each other again.'

'And what happens the next time one of your family tries to matchmake?' she reasoned impatiently.

He smiled at her confidently. 'Just because the two of us don't intend seeing each other again after this weekend, it doesn't mean my family have to be made aware of the fact. I think a relationship between the two of us—purely fictional, of course—should be good for six months or so. After which I'm hoping my matchmaking mama will be so engrossed in being a grandmother to Wolf's son or daughter that she will lose all interest in finding me a wife!'

He had it all worked out, didn't he? Darci thought crossly.

Except, as she knew to her cost, the best-laid plans didn't always work the way one expected....

'A little overwhelming, isn't it?' The tall and beautiful Angel Gambrelli laughed sympathetically as Darci stared at the two men who stood together across the room, preparing drinks for them all.

Luc and his brother, Wolf.

They were both tall, both blond-haired—although Luc's overlong hair was a deeper gold than his brother's—and their aristocratically handsome faces very similar, as were the powerfully muscled bodies beneath their black evening suits and white shirts.

Having been introduced to Luc's brother and his wife when they'd arrived at the suite a couple of minutes ago, Darci still couldn't get over the sensory shock of having two such forcefully attractive men as the Gambrelli brothers together in the same room!

'Believe me, it doesn't get any easier, either,' Angel continued conversationally as she looked at her husband with adoring eyes, her long dark hair loose down her spine, the red dress she wore not disguising the slight swell of her pregnancy. 'And you haven't even met Cesare yet!' she added knowingly. 'A tall, dark, brooding Sicilian,' she warned with another sympathetic smile, before turning to thank her husband as he brought their drinks over.

Darci pondered as she took her own glass of champagne from Luc. 'I really don't think I can do this, Luc,' she muttered, feeling distinctly uncomfortable in her strappy black dress, with its low neckline and three-inches-above-the-knee length, when Angel Gambrelli looked so beautiful in her elegant designer label red dress.

Usually cool and calm under pressure, Darci knew that her normal self-confidence had taken a distinct knock when the other couple had arrived minutes ago, looking so suavely sophisticated.

It didn't help that she and Luc had had a blazing row earlier, when Darci had discovered the suite only had one bedroom!

The fact that Luc had shrugged off her anger with the comment that their relationship would hardly look convincing to his family if they occupied separate bedrooms hadn't appeased her fury in the slightest. Neither had his assurances that he had every intention of sleeping on the couch in the sitting-room.

How was she supposed to sleep tonight knowing that Luc was only feet away on the couch in the adjoining room?

Although the fact that this was the first time they had even spoken to each other since they'd had the row would probably ensure that Darci continued to say little, as Luc had requested earlier; it was the smile that might prove a little more difficult to achieve!

Luc took a much-needed sip of his champagne. Much needed because his usually unshakable self-control had taken a distinct knock the moment Darci had appeared in the sitting-room, shortly before Wolf and Angel arrived, wearing a black dress that revealed more than it covered.

Dear God, he reflected now. She looked so sexy he wanted to rip the dress away and feast himself on the body that he was pretty sure was virtually naked beneath the clinging black material!

The blackness of his mood wasn't improved by the fact that one glance at Wolf's amused expression told him that his brother knew exactly what line his thoughts had taken.

What every red-blooded man at the party tonight would also be thinking every time he so much as looked at Darci. And Luc had no doubt that plenty of them—that all of his male relatives—would be looking!

'Maybe you should have worn something a little less—revealing. You might feel more comfortable,' he observed sardonically. And instantly felt like a complete bastard as he saw the hurt in Darci's expressive green eyes when she looked up at him reproachfully. 'You look beautiful,' he assured her, with soft impatience at the fact that he wanted to take off his evening jacket and wrap it concealingly around the bareness of Darci's shoulders, the full swell of her breasts revealed above the low neckline of the dress that Luc was certain only just covered the tempting rosy tips of her succulent nipples. God, he could almost taste—

'Don't try and be nice to me, Luc—I know I look distinctly underdressed!' Darci came back forcefully, her fingers gripping her champagne glass so tightly that her knuckles showed white as she took another reviving sip of the wine.

'Goodness knows what Wolf and Angel will think of me,' she hissed angrily.

Luc could take a pretty shrewd guess at what his brother thought of Darci, having seen the unmistakable male admiration in Wolf's impersonal gaze as the two of them were introduced. And Angel, absolutely secure in her husband's love, obviously thought her beautiful, too.

'They like you,' Luc assured her honestly. 'Just stop fussing with it,' he advised her brusquely, as Darci attempted to pull the low neckline of the dress higher, only succeeding in giving him a tantalising glimpse of her rosy nipples instead. 'Don't you have a wrap or something you could wear?' he added harshly, annoyed at the stirring of his own arousal. The last thing he wanted was to go downstairs and present himself to his mother with his erection visibly throbbing!

'Yes, I do have a wrap. But it would look rather silly if I wear it when we're remaining in the hotel,' Darci came back reasoningly.

'I'll tell everyone you have a cold,' Luc retorted softly.

'My hero!' she came back witheringly.

'I'll be a lot more than that if you don't stop fidgeting and cover yourself up,' he warned darkly.

Darci stilled her restless movements to look searchingly up at Luc, easily seeing the heat in his gaze as it remained riveted on the creamy swell of her breasts, a nerve pulsing in his tightly clenched jaw.

Luc looked more uncomfortable than she felt!

But for a totally different reason, Darci realised, as she couldn't help but notice the telltale signs of Luc's arousal.

Luc wanted her!

Which meant, despite all he had said when they'd had

dinner at Garstang's, and his indifference when they'd travelled from the U.K. earlier today, that Luc wasn't immune to her after all.

Strangely, that realisation helped her to calm down and relax. In fact, she could feel her self-confidence returning by the second—so much so that she felt almost…empowered.

Luc, for all that he might not want to feel that way, was still as attracted to her as he had been the first night they'd met, when he had described to her in detail how he would like to undress her and make love to her!

'Calm down, Luc,' she chided him knowingly. 'Or you'll give your brother and his wife totally the wrong impression about us,' she baited, knowing by the way his head snapped up and he turned to look at the other couple with slightly dazed eyes that, for the few minutes of their conversation, he had forgotten they weren't alone. 'And we wouldn't want that, now, would we?' she finished wryly.

Luc's mouth tightened ominously. 'Enjoy yourself while you can, Darci,' he warned darkly. 'But while you're doing so, just remember that when we return here later this evening you will be completely alone with me!'

His threat sent a thrill of anticipation down Darci's spine, rather than the trepidation she was sure Luc had meant her to feel!

CHAPTER TWELVE

'DO I HEAR the sound of wedding bells…?'

Luc turned to glare at his brother as Wolf came to stand beside him on the edge of the dance floor where, following their mother's sumptuous birthday party, a dozen or so couples amongst the fifty-odd guests were gyrating.

Darci and Cesare were one of those couples….

'Not unless you have tinnitus,' Luc came back with terse dismissal.

Wolf laughed softly. 'The family all like your little Darci,' he observed lightly.

'She isn't little.' At least not in certain places, Luc thought with an inward groan, as he felt the unwanted aching throb of his body. He could picture those places. That minuscule black dress was leaving very little to the imagination! 'Neither is she mine,' he added with vigour.

'No?' Wolf took a sip of his wine as he glanced across to where Darci was dancing in Cesare's assured arms. 'Then why did you bring her here?' He was looking curious when his gaze returned to Luc.

Luc grimaced. 'Because if I hadn't, either you, or Cesare—or worse, Mamma—would only have spent this evening introducing me to one eligible—marriageable—female after another!' Luc could see half a dozen or so of them in the room even now. All beautiful and no doubt accomplished women who left him completely cold.

'You have it all wrong there, little brother,' Wolf corrected. 'The matchmaking is completely the girls' idea; Cesare and I know better.'

Luc scowled darkly. 'Meaning?'

His brother sighed. 'Meaning that I spent years trying to avoid the Gambrelli Curse of falling so deeply in love with a woman that to contemplate life without her was unthinkable. In fact, I was probably the biggest playboy in Europe—okay, I *was* the biggest playboy in Europe,' he conceded dryly, at Luc's scathing glance, giving one of those vulpine smiles that had helped in his being known to the world as Wolf Gambrelli. 'But when it actually happened, there wasn't a damn thing I could do about it. It was the same for Cesare. Neither of us was actively *looking* for the women we were fated to love— in fact, the opposite!—but along they came anyway. And you know what, Luc…?' He smiled again, with no hint of wolfishness at all. 'Once I had stopped fighting the whole idea of loving, once I had accepted that my life had absolutely no meaning without Angel in it, I was only too happy to capitulate to fate.'

'I'm not,' Luc declared adamantly. 'And no amount of matchmaking on the girls' part is going to change that! Because what none of them seem to have grasped is that I am perfectly happy with my unmarried state!'

'Really?' Wolf drawled, with another speculative glance in Darci's direction.

Luc felt a tightening of his stomach muscles as he turned

in the same direction, just in time to see Darci laughing at something Cesare had said, her beautiful face glowing as she looked up at him, her eyes a warm, beguiling green.

This evening hadn't gone quite as planned, Luc acknowledged resignedly. He had imagined it would just be a question of having Darci at his side to act as a buffer against his family's matchmaking, leaving him free to enjoy his mother's birthday party. Tomorrow, after he had returned Darci to London, he would be on his way back to his carefree—commitment-free!—life in Los Angeles.

In none of his calculations had he taken into account the fact that he had to get through this evening in the disturbing company of a sexily alluring Darci before that could happen. Or that, as Wolf had just pointed out, the whole of his family would actually like and approve of Darci….

Although why the latter hadn't occurred to him, Luc had no idea; everything about Darci was attractive—from her unmistakable beauty to her sharp intelligence and the warmth of her personality.

'Really,' he assured Wolf vehemently, before turning away to once again look at Darci from beneath hooded lids. 'So just tell the girls to back off, will you?' he requested, with firm determination.

Darci, moving lightly and easily to the music in Cesare Gambrelli's arms, was nevertheless totally aware of Luc's brooding presence as he stood talking to his brother on the edge of the dance floor. It would be a little difficult *not* to be aware of Luc when he was staring at her so intently!

The evening had become less traumatic for Darci once they'd got downstairs to the reception room, where the party was being held, and she'd seen several other women wearing dresses even more revealing than her own—giving her a breathing space in which to get over her initial nervousness.

Totally prepared by Angel's warning, she had been introduced to Cesare—and to the impact of having three devastatingly handsome Gambrelli men in the same room.

Cesare's wife, Robin, had been as warm and friendly as Darci had found Angel earlier—these two marriages were obviously a success, if the warm intimacy between the respective husbands and wives was any indication. And Darci was pretty sure that it was.

Luc's mother, Chantelle Gambrelli—French, and the obvious matriarch of the Gambrelli family—had been much more of a surprise.

Very petite, and still incredibly beautiful—even though aged in her early sixties—she had all the chic her French nationality implied. Her knee-length dress was the same shade of blue as her eyes, and her blonde hair was worn smooth and straight to her slender shoulders—Darci had wondered where the hair colour of the two Sicilian brothers had come from! Chantelle nevertheless ruled her family with a charming but indomitable will.

A formidable will, Darci would have said—which explained why Luc had been so determined to thwart his mother's efforts, at least this weekend, to find her younger son a wife!

'Have you and Luc known each other very long?' Cesare Gambrelli's husky, slightly accented voice prompted politely as they danced.

It seemed like for ever to Darci—her life was going to seem very empty without Luc in it after this weekend together!— but in reality it really had been only a matter of days.

'Not really, no,' she answered, lightly but unhelpfully.

'Hmm,' Cesare murmured dryly.

Darci looked up at him as she sensed there was more behind his response. 'Sorry…?'

Cesare—tall, dark and incredibly handsome—elaborated. 'Luc does not seem his usual relaxed and charming self this evening.'

Darci knew that Luc hadn't been the 'relaxed and charming' man she had initially met at the premiere of Grant's film well before coming to this party this evening—knew this change in Luc had occurred earlier in the week, when he had realised how she had deliberately manipulated him into asking her out just so that she could exact her revenge on him for the way he had hurt Mellie. For the way she had *believed* he'd hurt Mellie!

A mistake for which Luc had exacted his own revenge, in turn, by making her feel guilty enough that she had agreed to come to Paris with him this weekend….

'He seems perfectly fine to me,' she dismissed.

'Really?' Cesare prompted as the music came to an end. His hand rested lightly beneath Darci's elbow as they turned to walk back to the table where Chantelle, Angel and Robin were seated.

'Yes, really,' Darci assured him, a slight blush in her cheeks as she looked up and found herself the focus of Cesare Gambrelli's dark, penetrating gaze.

They did have the most intense, compelling brown eyes, these Gambrelli men, Darci allowed as she felt her blush deepening at the deliberate lie; Luc didn't seem fine to her at all!

He was moody, bad-tempered, and had virtually growled at her earlier, when she'd initially appeared in the sitting-room in her revealing black dress, making her more self-conscious of her appearance then ever.

Of course, his mood could be due to the argument that had ensued when she had discovered there was only one bedroom in their hotel suite....

'My dance, I believe?' Luc demanded as he joined them, his gaze narrowing on the delicate colour in Darci's cheeks before he turned questioningly to his cousin.

Cesare smiled confidently back at him. 'Darci is a wonderful dancer,' he confirmed.

Luc's eyes narrowed to dark slits. 'Darci is wonderful at a lot of things,' he snapped, and then immediately regretted his testiness as he heard Darci's sharply indrawn breath. Feeling even worse when he looked down and saw the hurt and reproach in her moss-green gaze, he amended, 'I meant, of course, that she's a very gifted and dedicated doctor.'

Cesare gave an inclination of his head, his mouth tight with disapproval. 'Of course you did,' he drawled. 'I hope we may dance together again later this evening, Darci.' His tone softened warmly as he relinquished his hold on her elbow before nodding abruptly to Luc and moving away to rejoin his wife.

Darci's face was slightly pale now, Luc noted with guilty impatience. 'I'm sorry,' he muttered as he drew her out onto the dance floor and took her in his arms. 'I'm afraid that at the moment being with my family has this effect on me,' he explained as they circled the floor.

'Really?' she came back tartly. 'I thought it was only me who had such a mood-changing effect on you!'

Luc's gaze was guarded as he looked down at her. 'Why do you say that?'

Darci's expression was challenging as she flicked back the

long length of her fiery-red hair to look up at him, baring the tops of her creamy breasts.

Darci's dress had been doing strange things to him all evening, Luc remembered, its low neckline and thin shoulder straps leaving far too much of her visible for his comfort even as the black material clung to the curve of her hips and narrow waist and exposed an expanse of her breasts. It didn't help that Luc could recall that her nipples were a tempting rosy pink....

'Let's just say you've been less than your charming self the last few hours,' she pointed out to him.

'You weren't exactly your charming self earlier this evening, either,' he reminded her, referring to the argument the two of them had had before Wolf and Angel had arrived.

'You know exactly why that was,' Darci retorted.

Yes, Luc knew exactly why that was....

Darci had disappeared to take her shower, only to come blazing back out of the bedroom seconds later, the light of battle in her sparkling green eyes.

Luc hadn't been sure whether to feel insulted or flattered when she had seemed less than reassured by his assertion that the arrangement was only for the benefit of his over-interested family—that he had every intention of sleeping on the couch in the sitting-room.

He had begun to doubt that assertion himself when she'd appeared in the sitting-room, minutes before Wolf and Angel were due to arrive, wearing this scandalously revealing dress that had the effect of totally demolishing his usual cool control!

She really did look incredibly beautiful this evening, and the swaying movements of her body as they danced, those wonderful breasts and lean hips occasionally brushing against him, was doing very little to still the clamouring of his senses.

He drew her a little closer to him, moulding her hips against his. Darci gave him a startled look as she obviously became aware of his arousal. 'Why don't we forget our argument of earlier, Darci?' he encouraged throatily. 'And just relax for the rest of this evening while we enjoy the romance that is Paris?'

Darci didn't dare allow herself to relax around this man— let alone allow the romance of the Parisian evening to invade and seduce her senses!

Although she knew that might prove a little difficult when Luc took advantage of an open door to dance her outside onto a deserted terrace. Her breath caught in her throat as Luc took her hand in his to draw her over to a more private corner and look across the rippling reflections on the Seine to the magnificence of the Eiffel Tower, illuminated by the hundreds and hundreds of lights that shrouded the steel structure in wonder and beauty.

'It's beautiful, isn't it?' she breathed softly.

'Very beautiful,' Luc murmured huskily.

Darci turned to look at him, her cheeks becoming warm, her mouth dry, as she found that Luc was looking at her rather than the lit-up landmark.

She shook her head. 'I don't think—'

'No—don't think!' he advised gruffly, his eyes darkly compelling as he took the step that brought his body close to hers.

His heat, his overwhelming sensuality, at once invaded her already raw and battered senses as his arms drew her even closer.

Darci couldn't breathe, couldn't speak as she lost herself in the mesmerising dark depths of his eyes seconds before he bent his head slightly and his mouth claimed hers in a kiss that was both searing and seductive.

It was too much for her to resist after days of only knowing Luc's scathing anger and cold displeasure, and her lips parted beneath Luc's even as her body instinctively curved into his much harder contours, his hard arousal pressing against the welcoming softness of her abdomen.

It was heaven to be kissed by Luc again, to allow herself to relax in his arms, to feel his lips and tongue exploring her, tasting her, as if he couldn't get enough of her.

Luc drew his lips from Darci's to trail a path of fire, of desire, down the column of her throat. 'I've been wanting to do this ever since you appeared earlier in that scandalous dress—'

'It isn't scandalous,' she groaned protestingly.

'No?' he prompted teasingly as he looked down at the fullness of her creamy breasts. 'What, exactly, are you wearing beneath it?' he pressed huskily.

'Exactly?' she echoed ruefully.

'Exactly.' He nodded, his eyes very dark.

Darci moistened her lips before answering, and Luc's heated gaze followed the sensual invitation. 'The dress is so clingy that I— Just a pair of panties,' she confided.

'Just a—!' Luc broke off, his breathing slightly ragged now. 'No wonder I'm far from the only man here tonight who can't take his eyes off you,' he said, knowing he hadn't been comfortable with other males even *looking* at her.

She blinked up at him. 'You can't take your eyes off me, Luc…?' she echoed.

'I can't look at anything else!' he confirmed, and his tongue tasted her perfumed skin, his teeth gently nibbling, moving, so that his body was shielding hers completely as one of his hands moved to cup one of those tempting breasts and he felt her body quiver in response to the intimacy.

Her breast fitted perfectly in his hand, her skin so smooth

and creamy. His fingers dipped beneath the clinging material and he ran them over the sensitive tip of her breast, his mouth moving up to once again capture hers as she groaned her pleasure at his caresses.

She felt so good, so full and heavy—her nipple thrusting tight and rigid against the palm of his hand, her mouth hot and moist as he thrust his tongue deep inside.

He wanted to touch her bare skin, needed to feel her heat against him. He pressed her back against the balustrade to move between her slightly parted legs, slipping the straps of her gown down to let the soft material of the dress fall to her waist. He bared her breasts to him, before stroking the soft pad of his thumb across the tautness of her nipple, feeling Darci's arousal as she moved her thighs against him in silent entreaty. Her lips parted wider for his kiss, and his tongue thrust even deeper inside her mouth, possessing her, claiming her, as he moved the hardness of his erection restlessly against her increasing heat.

'I want you, Darci!' he exclaimed hotly, as his lips left hers to trail a path of fire down the creamy column of her throat to the curve of those creamy breasts, before dipping lower and laying claim to her other thrusting nipple, drawing its stiffness into his mouth and suckling hungrily.

Could she take this one evening—one night? Darci wondered longingly. She knew herself totally lost to Luc's kisses and caresses. Could she just allow the romance of the evening, the deep love she felt for Luc, to take over? To lose herself in the desire she now knew without a doubt that he still felt for her? Could she take all that Luc had to give and give back to him in return?

How could she not give in to that need when she was on

fire for him? The ache created in her body by his lips, hands and mouth was deepening to breaking point as she felt the relentlessness of his lips against her breast, the silky rasp of his tongue against her nipple, and her groans were now of impending release.

Her hands moved to cradle the back of his head as she pressed herself against him, increasing the pressure of those marauding lips and tongue, knowing Luc was aware of her imminent release. He growled low in his throat and his thighs began to move in stroking, sensuous rhythm against hers, making her wet and open as she felt the fierce fire of growing sexual arousal between her legs.

'Touch me, Darci!' He let her go to groan achingly. 'For God's sake, touch me!'

She needed no second invitation—had been longing to touch, to feel him for days, it seemed. Her hand moved down to gently grasp the hard length of him, stroking him first softly and then more firmly as she felt the leap of his erection straining against her caressing hand.

But it wasn't enough—not nearly enough. Darci wanted to touch skin-to-skin, groaning her satisfaction as she released the button on his trousers to slowly move the zip downwards before her hand dipped inside to curl around his silky hardness, moving against him, around him, in the same rhythm as Luc had suckled her breast, feeling the beads of moisture at the very tip of his sensitive length as he gasped his own threatening release.

'No more, Darci!' he protested, as he moved back slightly, gently dislodging her hand and then removing it completely. 'Not like this,' he explained tenderly at her look of disappointment. 'I want to be inside you,' he urged. 'I want— Just let me love you for now,' he insisted, and once again he moved between her legs to press his manhood against her before his mouth moved to claim her breast.

His hand increased the pressure on her other nipple now, squeezing, sending quivers of sensation downwards, burning her, wetting her as she moved rhythmically against him, her head going back, her neck arching, as the fire engulfed and claimed her, sending spasm after spasm of relentless pleasure through and over her as she exploded against his thrusting flesh.

Luc's hand moved down between them as he continued to lave her breast, and his fingers unerringly found the hardened nub of her arousal through the damp satin of her underwear, rubbing, pressing, increasing in intensity as he gave her the orgasm he had so cruelly denied her on Tuesday afternoon. The pleasure seemed never-ending, and Darci felt as if she were shattering into a million pieces.

Her head dropped forward onto Luc's shoulder, her fingers clinging tightly to him as those waves of release finally began to subside, her breath coming in short, breathy gasps as she fought to regain control of her senses. For a while they just held one another, then Luc pulled away to rearrange their clothing before taking her back in his arms.

'Luc, *chéri*, I do not think that this is quite the right time or place for—*amour*,' murmured a huskily amused voice that Darci instantly recognised as belonging to Chantelle Gambrelli.

Darci buried her face even deeper against Luc's shoulder to shield her embarrassment, mortified colour burning her cheeks as she realised the two of them had actually been making love on the terrace of one of the public rooms of the Gambrelli Hotel!

CHAPTER THIRTEEN

'DARCI, we can't leave yet!' Luc implored her, as he caught up with her in the reception area of the hotel to grasp her arm and turn her to face him.

Her eyes blazed deeply green. 'You can't,' she accepted. 'But I certainly can!'

Luc returned her gaze frustratedly. 'My mother didn't see anything—'

'She didn't need to see anything,' Darci came back emotionally. 'It had to be pretty obvious even to the most casual observer—which your mother most certainly isn't!—exactly what we were doing.'

When Chantelle Gambrelli had interrupted the two of them, Darci's reaction had been to turn and run through and from the room where the party was being held. She had been made all the more desperate because, having come back to reality with the suddenness of being dunked in a cold shower, she had been completely unnerved by the realisation of the intensity of her own hunger.

Her life had been so structured up to this point—with her goals and ambitions not quite set in stone, but close enough. She had wanted to be a doctor, the very best doctor she could be, and personal relationships of any kind had necessarily been put on hold until she had achieved that goal.

The fact that none of that had seemed important while Luc was kissing and caressing her, that she had forgotten everything but him and the feel of his mouth and hands on her body, everything but touching him as intimately, shook her to the core.

She loved Luc. She had already known that before she'd agreed to come away with him this weekend, but until a few minutes ago she hadn't realised the depth of that love, how it nullified, made less of everything that made up the fabric of her life.

The love she had for Luc was mind-consuming, as well as emotion-consuming; he possessed and captured her to the exclusion of all and everything else.

But Luc had no intention of returning that depth of emotion. He had made it clear that he totally denied love in his life.

Oh, Darci had no doubt that after this evening Luc might consider offering her an affair. But just the thought of becoming one of those needy, clinging women who only lived for the intermittent visits of her lover made Darci feel cold inside.

Loving Luc as she did, she didn't think she could ever settle for so little of him....

Luc looked down at Darci as the emotions flickered across her expressive face far too quickly for him to read, let alone analyse. 'Darci, talk to me!' he urged as he held her gently in front of him.

She shook her head, her gaze no longer meeting his. 'Just now was a mistake. An embarrassing mistake,' she recalled with a quiver. 'And I really can't face your mother again after—after that.' She sighed wearily. 'Could you please make my excuses to the rest of your family?'

It was only ten-thirty—far too early, in all politeness, for

Luc to absent himself from his own mother's birthday party. And, after the intimacy of the scene his mother had witnessed a few minutes ago, only one construction could be put on both Darci and himself disappearing now!

He didn't want his family to think those things of Darci, of all women....

She already looked what she was: a woman who had just reached the peak of sexual arousal. Her eyes were still slightly misty from her release, her mouth kiss-swollen, her dress slightly crumpled from where he had pushed it out of the way with impatient hands, so that he might touch and caress her naked breasts.

None of which would have been missed minutes ago by his over-interested family as Darci had made her hasty exit, closely followed by a darkly scowling Luc!

He released her to nod abruptly, knowing the reception area of the hotel wasn't the place for this discussion. 'I will tell my family that you have a headache and have retired to bed.'

Darci looked up at him with shadowed eyes. 'Do you think that what your mother witnessed just now will convince her to back off with her matchmaking?'

He shrugged broad shoulders, his face an expressionless mask. 'Let's just say that your presence tonight has—served its purpose.'

She gave a tight smile. 'Thank goodness we're due to leave early tomorrow morning! I don't think I could face any of your family again after tonight,' she added, at Luc's questioning look.

'Don't worry about that just now, Darci.'

'Don't *worry* about it?' she echoed with a pained wince. 'I'm never going to be able to forget it!'

'I will explain everything to my family,' Luc reassured her.

Explain what? Darci wondered. That she was just another woman, like all the other women he had ever been involved with? That she meant no more to him than any of them had?

What did it matter what explanation Luc gave his family about her? After tonight, Darci knew she wouldn't see them— or Luc—ever again!

'Go up to bed, Darci,' Luc encouraged gently. 'I will join you shortly.'

She frowned at how intimate that sounded. 'I'll leave some blankets and pillows in the sitting-room for you,' she told him wearily.

Luc gave a teasing smile. 'You still want me to sleep on the couch…?'

'I do,' she assured him firmly; she needed to be alone right now, completely alone, in order to sort out the jumbled messages in her brain.

Her body was telling her that she still wanted Luc, that it would be oh-so-easy to have this one night with him. But her head was telling her that once would never be enough, and that even if Luc were to offer her a little more than that—an affair until his interest in her waned—she would only be opening herself up to indescribable pain if she gave in to that temptation.

Luc's smile faded at her adamant tone. He knew that he wasn't mistaken in his belief that only minutes ago Darci had wanted him as fully as he had wanted her.

That fierce need, that complete lack of control, was something that had never happened to Luc before….

He drew in a ragged breath. 'Darci, I think that you and I need to talk—'

'I can't imagine what about,' she dismissed briskly. 'Besides, I really do have a headache now,' she informed him flatly.

'I thought it was only married ladies who developed headaches at bedtime?' he replied.

'That's a generalisation I very much doubt is true of Robin or Angel,' she came back tartly.

No, Luc was sure that it wasn't. He had absolutely no doubts as to the compatibility of his brother and cousin with their wives. 'Darci—'

'You really should get back to the party now, Luc,' Darci told him firmly.

Yes, he knew he should. But he also knew that he and Darci needed to talk. Had to talk. Tonight.

Darci had withdrawn from him in the last few minutes, had developed a wariness towards him that Luc simply couldn't allow to continue.

Not now....

His mouth tightened determinedly. 'I will join you in a few minutes,' he stated evenly.

She nodded abruptly. 'Try not to disturb me if I'm asleep, hmm?'

Luc's eyes narrowed as he acknowledged that Darci had the ability to disturb *him* even when he was asleep!

He had thought of little and certainly no one else since he'd met her ten days ago, he realised now. He was able to feel the creamy warmth of her skin beneath his fingers, taste her silken flesh, even when they were apart.

'You're a junior doctor, Darci—you must be used to going without sleep,' he came back purposefully.

Darci eyed him warily, not completely sure how she was going to deal with this situation. Luc certainly wasn't going to believe, after her total loss of control on the terrace, that she didn't want him!

She shook her head. 'It's because I'm a junior doctor that I need to get all the sleep I can when I have the opportunity.'

That warm brown gaze roamed slowly over her flushed face, lingering on her kiss-swollen lips before once again moving up to capture her startled green eyes with his. 'Tonight isn't going to be one of those opportunities,' he assured her.

'The two of us going to bed together wasn't part of our bargain, Luc,' Darci told him.

He shrugged broad shoulders. 'Our original *bargain*, as you call it, is at an end.'

'Just like that?' Darci challenged indignantly. 'Because you've decided that it is?'

Luc's mouth quirked wryly as he easily guessed her intent. 'Darci, I believe you are deliberately trying to provoke yet another argument between the two of us.'

'I'm not trying to do anything—we *are* having an argument!' she assured him heatedly. 'You seem to be under the delusion that a few kisses on a hotel terrace while I was seduced by the romance of Paris by moonlight entitles you to share my bed tonight—'

'It wasn't Paris by moonlight that seduced you, Darci.' Luc's voice had hardened impatiently. 'Any more than it was the moonlight that seduced me,' he continued more gently. 'Darci, no matter what I may have said to you previously, you must now realise that I have no intention of saying goodbye to you at the end of this weekend.'

'You won't have any choice in the matter,' she cut in decisively. 'I already have a very full life, Luc, and I certainly don't have any room in it for a rich Sicilian playboy who might have decided he wants to hop in and out of my bed whenever he happens to be in London!' She glared at him stubbornly.

Luc's eyes narrowed to icy slits even as he acknowledged that Darci's accusation might be true—*was* true!—of all his previous relationships.

'It is exactly because you have these sort of prejudices where I'm concerned that the two of us need to talk,' he placated huskily.

'Before or after we've gone to bed together?' Darci retorted.

'That, my dear Darci, is entirely up to you,' he drawled.

Really, the arrogance of the man—to believe that her capitulation earlier entitled him to think he could now instigate an affair with her!

A relationship which, loving him as deeply as she did, Darci knew could never be the light-hearted affair for her that it would be to Luc....

'I'm sorry, Luc, but I don't do affairs,' she told him, before turning sharply on her heel and walking away from him towards the lift.

Totally aware of Luc's dark gaze on her back every step of the way!

He was still standing where Darci had left him when she turned, once inside the lift, and pressed the button to ascend. His expression was unreadable, his gaze enigmatic, and Darci only breathed again when the lift doors closed on him.

What was she going to do? she wondered desperately as the lift went up.

She loved Luc. Of that she had absolutely no doubt.

Just as there was no doubting, from what he had said just now, that Luc desired her enough to initiate an affair.

An affair that Darci had once believed she would accept, if it was ever offered, but now knew that she couldn't.

Just as she also knew that she wouldn't be able to resist Luc if he should make love to her again....

Something she was pretty sure was going to happen when he rejoined her in the suite.

Again she asked herself what she was going to do.

She could just take tonight and then tell him tomorrow that there would be no affair.

Except that one night with Luc would never be enough.

Even a week, a month, two months wouldn't be enough!

Tonight she had realised that the love she felt for Luc was so overpowering, so deeply a part of her, that only a lifetime with him would assuage the need she had for him.

And, just as she didn't 'do' affairs, Luc had made it obvious he didn't 'do' lifetime commitment....

CHAPTER FOURTEEN

DARCI didn't prepare for bed once she got back to the suite. Instead she changed into the denims she had worn to travel over in earlier today, and a fitted black T-shirt, before moving to sit curled up in the window seat in the sitting-room, wrapping her arms about her bent knees as she stared sightlessly out of the window and prepared to sit and wait for Luc to return from the party.

She had realised Luc was right as she'd flung the seductive black dress back into her suitcase—with an inward vow never to wear it again!—they *did* need to talk. And the sooner Luc accepted that she wouldn't enter into an affair with him the better it would be for both of them.

Although, again, she knew Luc was going to be very hard to resist if he should attempt to seduce her into capitulating....

Darci had never realised, never guessed, that loving someone, loving Luc, could be so totally, so emotionally consuming, that she didn't seem to be able to think of anything else but him.

It almost made her understand why Mellie had resorted to subterfuge in order to try and attract Grant's attention!

Almost....

Because, no matter how much she might love him, Darci

knew she would never be tempted to such deception in order to have Luc permanently in her life.

She stiffened tensely as she heard the key-card in the lock seconds before the door handle turned, her heart beating faster, the palms of her hands suddenly damp as she knew that, even though it was still only eleven o'clock, Luc was back.

He certainly hadn't lingered downstairs for any longer than he absolutely had to, had he?

Luc saw Darci's silhouette on the window seat as soon as his gaze had adjusted to the gloom of the unlit sitting-room. Her hair gleamed like fire against the bright moonlight behind her, and he was convinced by her wary stillness that the lack of light in the room was a deliberate move on her part.

That was okay with him; a blaze of bright lights wasn't exactly conducive to what he had to say anyway.

And he should have known that Darci, once she had thought the situation over, no matter what she might have said to the contrary earlier, wouldn't just go to bed and cower beneath the bedclothes, hoping Luc wouldn't disturb her. After all, she was the type of woman who believed in facing a challenge head-on.

Except he was no longer the challenge—*she* was!

'Darci,' he greeted her quietly as he came across the room to join her. He was slightly disappointed that she had changed out of the scandalous black dress—he could imagine nothing more erotic than slowly peeling it from her delectable body!— but at the same time knew it would probably have been too much of a distraction. He had every intention of the two of them talking before—well, before anything else.

She steadily returned his gaze. 'Luc,' she returned economically.

No help there, he acknowledged ruefully. But no doubt she was still unsettled—upset—about what had happened on the terrace earlier.

Upset wasn't quite the word Luc would have used concerning his own feelings about making love to Darci earlier. *Enlightened* probably best described how he now felt....

Why didn't Luc just get this conversation over with? Darci fretted inwardly, as he remained silent while he continued to look down at her with those enigmatic dark eyes. Why didn't Luc just make the offer of an affair she was sure he was going to make, hear her refusal, and then let her escape to the privacy of the bedroom?

Where she could bury her head under the bedcovers so that he shouldn't hear her crying her heart out!

Especially as, now that she was with Luc again, a part of her—a large part of her—wished, longed to accept the offer!

It was going to be the hardest thing she had ever done in her life, loving Luc as she did, to turn and walk away from him.

But perhaps this was her punishment for all the times she had held herself aloof, apart, from any idea of emotional involvement? For all the times she had walked away without a second glance when a man she had agreed to go out with once or twice showed more than a passing interest in her? In some cases it had been a most decided interest, but she had remained immune, leaving a string of broken hearts behind her, as Kerry had once put it.

But Darci hadn't deliberately set out to hurt any of those men. She had simply had her sights set on her career to the exclusion of all else....

Whatever her intention, it was obvious that the fates decreed that when she finally did fall in love, it would be with someone who was as elusive, as unobtainable, as she had been herself the last ten years!

Her mouth firmed and she shook her head. 'I meant what I said earlier, Luc. I am not going to sleep with you tonight.'

'I can assure you that sleep is the last thing I have on my mind,' he drawled in amusement, as he moved to sit at the other end of the window seat.

She gave him a reproving look. 'Don't tease, Luc.'

He returned her gaze consideringly. 'But it has become one of my pleasures in life to tease you, Darci,' he murmured.

She glared. 'It's a pleasure you'll have to forgo in future!'

'You don't want me?' He frowned.

Darci was glad of the darkness to hide the blush in her cheeks. 'I can hardly claim that after what happened earlier!'

'Then where is the problem?' he mused.

'The problem is I don't—'

'Do affairs,' he finished dryly.

'Exactly,' she said with satisfaction. 'And as you don't do anything else *but* affairs— Luc, what are you doing?' she gasped, slightly breathless as his lean fingers slid caressingly along the bareness of her foot to her ankle and then back again, sending shivers of awareness along the length of her leg and up into her already sensitised groin.

Luc continued to caress the lean beauty of her foot, knowing by the sudden unevenness of Darci's breathing that she was as disturbed by his touch as he was by the feel of her silky skin against his fingertips.

How or why this had happened to him had ceased to be important, Luc realised ruefully. Darci was all that was important now. And, no matter how she protested, he couldn't let her just walk out of his life!

But knowing that Darci wanted him physically, that she responded to his kisses and caresses, did not mean that she felt anything else for him but desire. And even that desire could not persuade her into going to bed with him....

He looked up at her, his dark gaze intense on the pale beauty of her face in the moonlight. 'Can you deny that you like my hands on your body, Darci?' he probed.

She swallowed hard, green eyes haunted. 'I haven't tried to deny it, Luc.' She sighed. 'I've simply told you that I won't have an affair with you.'

'Yes, I believe you have made it very clear that you do not have any room in your life for "a rich Sicilian playboy who might have decided he wants to hop in and out of your bed whenever he happens to be in London"!' Luc acknowledged hardly.

The fact that Luc remembered what she had said earlier told Darci that her remark must have hit a raw nerve. But why should it have done? She was no more conversant with affairs than she was with relationships, but wasn't the behaviour Luc had just described exactly what his relationships involved?

'What if I were to offer you more than an affair, Darci?' he said abruptly.

She became suddenly still, her expression wary. 'Such as...?' she prompted guardedly.

Luc gave a self-derisive smile as he shrugged. 'What is the next progression on from an affair, Darci?'

Darci looked at him frowningly, trying to read something—anything!—from his expression, and failing utterly. Luc's face was an unreadable mask, only the dark glitter of his eyes betraying any emotion at all. And she had no idea what that emotion was!

She moistened dry lips. 'You're suggesting I move in with

you while the attraction lasts?' She shook her head. 'That would no more work than an affair, when you live in Los Angeles and I live in London,' she reasoned.

Really, why didn't he just give this up and stop causing her any more heartache? she wondered tremblingly.

His eyes narrowed. 'You would not consider transferring your place of work to Los Angeles?'

'No, I would not,' she dismissed tersely, turning to swing her legs to the floor before standing up and moving impatiently away from those caressing fingers. 'Any more than you would consider transferring *your* place of work to London,' she added, as she moved away to pace restlessly.

Luc watched her movements, admiring the lean strength of her body, the way that luxurious red hair moved silkily down the length of her spine. 'Why don't you try asking me?' he suggested.

She stopped her pacing to stare across at him suspiciously. 'What game are you playing now, Luc?'

He gave a rueful smile. 'No game, Darci. Ask me.' His smile faded as he pressed her determinedly.

'Just so that you can say no?' she replied, shaking her head. 'I don't think so, Luc—'

'Ask me, damn you!' he bit out impatiently.

He hadn't expected this to be so difficult, Luc admitted frustratedly. Perhaps if he knew how Darci felt about him he might feel more relaxed about the outcome of this conversation. But as he had absolutely no idea of her feelings, other than the desire that exploded between them every time they were together, he didn't feel he had any choice but to step cautiously.

'Okay, Luc.' She sighed. 'I'm asking.'

'What exactly are you asking?' he came back.

'Would you move the base of your work to London so that the two of us can live together?'

'Yes.'

Her face froze as she stared at him. 'Yes…?' she finally repeated faintly.

Luc gave a mocking inclination of his head. 'Yes,' he confirmed dryly.

'But— I— You— Don't be ridiculous!' she cried.

He gave a pained wince. 'What is so ridiculous about it, Darci? Wolf and Cesare have both moved their centre of business to the U.K., so that Angel and Robin might continue with their respective jobs. Angel is now a research assistant to a government politician; Robin is her father's assistant in their family publishing company.'

'They're both married,' Darci replied. 'People tend to make sacrifices like that when they're married. But not when they're conducting affairs,' she finished firmly, as Luc would have spoken. 'I'm sure you've never even thought about doing something like this before, just so that you can have an affair with someone!'

'True,' Luc acknowledged. 'But we would be living together, not conducting an affair,' he corrected.

'It's the same thing!' Darci declared stubbornly.

'No, it is not,' Luc responded succinctly, standing up slowly. His mouth firmed with displeasure as Darci automatically took a step away from him. 'Darci, I would be willing to move to London, to restrict to a minimum the amount of time I would need to go away on business, in order to be with you. What are *you* willing to give?' he asked, moving stealthily forward to stand in front of her, his dark gaze searching her set features.

Darci stared up at him frowningly, not knowing what this conversation was about—only aware that Luc was offering her a glimpse of heaven!

Perhaps if he did move to London, and the two of them did set up home together somewhere, Luc might eventually fall in love with her…?

No, he wouldn't, she answered herself almost instantly. Luc didn't intend falling in love with any woman. Ever. He had made that more than plain when he had told her of how his parents' love for each other had excluded Wolf and himself.

She shifted her gaze away from his and her shoulders slumped wearily. 'Nothing,' she told him in a whisper. 'I'm not willing to give anything in order to live with you, Luc. In London or anywhere else,' she said, so that there should be no misunderstanding between them.

He drew in a harsh breath. 'That is your final word on the subject?'

She nodded stiffly, her gaze fixed on the rapid rise and fall of his chest beneath his snowy-white evening shirt. 'My absolute, final word,' she confirmed breathlessly, knowing that medically hearts didn't really break—even if the pain in her chest told her otherwise! 'Please believe that I do appreciate the—that I realise it can't have been— Goodnight, Luc,' she muttered shakily, before she brushed past him and almost ran across to the bedroom, closing the door firmly behind her.

Luc stood where she had left him for several long, painful minutes as he fought for control, each heavy beat of his heart seeming to wrench through his chest as he faced the bitterness of knowing he had lost Darci.

No, he hadn't lost her—because Darci had never been his to lose!

He wouldn't accept that.

He *couldn't* accept that.

He wasn't going to give up without a fight, Luc decided fiercely, narrowing his eyes determinedly as he strode purposefully towards the bedroom.

CHAPTER FIFTEEN

DARCI looked up fearfully from where she lay face-down on the bed as she heard the bedroom door open and then close. Her vision was too blurred by tears for her to be able to see any more than the silhouette of Luc's tall imposing figure as he approached.

She knew that she wouldn't be strong enough, that she loved Luc too much to withstand another onslaught on her emotions....

The bed gave slightly as he sat down beside her to reach out and turn her over, to draw her into his arms, burying his face in her hair. Darci's own arms moved up instinctively about his shoulders and she clung on tight.

'Please understand that I just can't do this, Luc!' she sobbed as she burrowed her face against the hardness of his chest. 'I wish that I could—you've no idea how I wish that I could be one of those women who would be happy to take the affair, the living together, that you're offering!' she admitted emotionally. 'But I can't! You see, I've never— I haven't ever— I'd probably be a terrible disappointment to you, anyway,' she added with a sob.

Luc became very still, moving back slightly to look down

at her searchingly, his own emotions catching in his throat as he saw her tears and the becoming blush that had coloured her cheeks. 'Darci, are you telling me what I think you are?' he murmured gruffly.

She hesitated. 'That I'm a twenty-eight-year-old virgin?' She gave a self-derisive grimace. 'Yes, Luc, that's exactly what I'm telling you.' She gave a shaky smile. 'So, you see, you really wouldn't want to have an affair with someone as inexperienced as me!'

The emotions that surged through Luc at that moment were so overwhelming that he found he couldn't speak for several seconds. He had thought, half-guessed the day of the picnic, that Darci was so skittish because she was a virgin. But to know it was a fact...

'You're right, Darci. I don't want to have an affair with you,' he finally confirmed softly.

Darci's mouth trembled slightly. 'I didn't think that you would once you knew the truth,' she replied slowly.

Luc straightened, holding her away from him slightly. 'Darci, I realised after you walked away from me just now that I had forgotten to tell you one important thing. No—' he sighed, shaking his head firmly '—I did not forget.' His accent deepened along with his emotions. 'I did not tell you because I was still intent on protecting myself,' he admitted huskily. 'Darci, I was not completely honest with you just now. I do not want an affair with you. I do not want to live with you, either. At least, not unless—Darci, will you marry me?' He held his breath as he waited for her answer.

Darci stared at him—at his tightly clenched jaw, at the bright glitter of his eyes—totally unable to read anything from the harshness of his expression.

'Isn't that rather an extreme step just to get me into bed?' she asked.

He gave a small smile. 'Very extreme—if that was all I wanted,' he allowed. 'Darci, Wolf spoke to me earlier this evening. He explained to me how it was between him and Angel when they first met. How he came to realise that he could not live without her in his life. How he knew that he would do anything, *be* anything, if she would only stay with him,' he added fiercely.

Darci couldn't breathe—certainly couldn't have spoken if her life had depended on it!

Luc gave a self-derisive shake of his head. 'Darci Wilde—sweet, beautiful, maddening Darci Wilde,' he murmured softly as his hands moved up to cradle each side of her face and he looked down at her wonderingly. 'I've realised this evening that is *exactly* how I feel about you!'

She moistened dry lips. 'You do…?'

'I do,' he conceded. 'I love you, Darci. I love you to the point of distraction!' he declared shakily. 'I know with certainty that I will love you for a lifetime. I will love you beyond a lifetime. I love you now beyond everything and anything. I will never love anyone but you,' he vowed fiercely. 'I love—'

'Luc, I think I get the message!' Darci broke in, even as she stared up at him in wonder.

Luc loved her. He wanted to marry her.

'But I deceived you,' she reminded him achingly. 'I deliberately set out to—' She broke off as Luc put a silencing thumb over her lips.

'It does not matter,' he assured her. 'You were protecting your friend.'

'A friend who didn't need protecting,' she reminded him guiltily.

Luc loved her?

It seemed too miraculous to be true!

'You did not know that,' Luc dismissed firmly. 'You are a loyal and true friend, Darci, as you will be a loyal and true life partner.' He told her what he had known two days ago. 'Whereas my own life has been—' He broke off momentarily. 'I have never cared enough about anyone to even contemplate doing what you did, Darci. My own life has been one of selfish pleasure, of taking what I wanted and giving very little back—'

'Please don't talk like that, Luc,' Darci interrupted him.

'But it is the truth,' he insisted heavily, deeply aware of the fact that he had fallen in love, irrevocably in love, with a woman who hadn't even said she loved him. 'I was so determined that I wouldn't ever love any woman in the total, emotion-consuming way that my father did my mother, excluding my brother and me, that I barely brushed the surface of relationships. I preferred to remain detached from all emotional commitment. Meeting you, falling in love with you, loving you, has shown me how selfish I have always been.'

'Because you believed that loving someone, loving in the total way that your parents did, would somehow make you less? That it would control and possibly destroy you?' Darci said quietly. 'That it would certainly damage any children born into that relationship?'

Luc looked at her silently for several long seconds before slowly nodding. 'Yes,' he said finally, surprised at her astuteness after the little he had told her about his childhood. 'But that isn't true, is it, Darci?' he realised, knowing that to see

Darci big with his baby, to love and nurture their child together, would only expand and deepen the love he already felt for her.

Maybe that hadn't been true of his parents' marriage. But he had watched Cesare with his children this last week, and knew it to be true of his cousin's marriage. And he knew from watching Wolf and Angel together this evening that the same would be true when their baby was born, too.

If he could just have Darci, if she would only agree to become his wife, he knew without a doubt that any children they had together would be included in their love. He *wanted* children with her. Desperately wanted that.

'No, that would never be true of a child we had together, Luc,' she assured him. 'Our children will be an affirmation of our love for each other, Luc, not a threat to our own relationship,' she told him shyly.

Luc became very still as he stared down at her, as he looked deep into those expressive green eyes and saw—as he saw…

He drew in a sharp breath, his hands tightening against her cheeks as he looked down at her wonderingly. 'Darci, do you love me…?' he breathed softly, hardly daring to believe it could be true.

'I love you, Luc,' she confirmed, her eyes starting to glow as her hands moved up to tightly clasp his arms. 'I love you so much that I'm as terrified as you obviously are,' she admitted. 'Luc, do you think two people like us—two people who, for different reasons admittedly, have been avoiding love all their lives—could possibly find happiness, love together…?'

Luc breathed deeply, his heart beating rapidly in his chest. 'I think—I know—that we are perfect for each other!' he declared fiercely.

Darci smiled. 'So do I,' she choked. 'Oh, Luc, so do I!' she cried joyously, and she moved to press her lips warmly against his.

Luc's arms closed firmly around her as he returned that kiss, drinking from her, claiming her for his own. 'I realised as I watched you this evening, as I proudly saw you charm all of my family, as well as totally enchanting me,' he said, 'that I can't bear the thought of never seeing you again, never being with you again. You are the sun, the moon and the stars to me, Darci!' He groaned as his mouth left hers to travel the length of her throat. 'I will love you until my dying breath!'

Heaven, Darci acknowledged glowingly as she thought of all the years ahead of them—loving each other, having children together, then grandchildren, maybe even great-grandchildren if they were very lucky.

Absolute heaven....

'Kerry tried to warn me before Grant's premiere that my little plan for revenge might backfire on me,' Darci said some time later, cradled in Luc's arms and looking up at him as the two of them lay on the bed together.

Luc smiled warmly. 'I'm looking forward to meeting your flatmate,' he told her. 'To meeting both your flatmates.'

Darci grimaced. 'Paying you back really was all my own idea.'

He laughed softly, indulgently. 'Oh, I know that, you little firebrand!' He dropped a light, forgiving kiss on her brow. 'I intend thanking Mellie when I finally meet her, not chastising her. Without her intervention the two of us might never have spent enough time together to fall in love with each other.'

Darci reached up to smooth his frown away. 'I prefer to

think that we would,' she replied. Some things are just meant to be. We're one of those things,' she added simply.

Luc turned on his side, facing her. 'You really believe that, Darci?' he pressed warmly.

'With all my heart,' she assured him with certainty. 'I've been waiting my whole life for you, Luc. My whole life!' she repeated fervently, her arms tightening about him as her lips parted to receive his kiss.

Her whole body sang in response to his. To his hard chest against the softness of her breasts, his hard arousal pressed against the liquid fire of her thighs as her legs became entangled with his.

'No, Darci!' Luc breathed raggedly as he abruptly broke the kiss.

She looked up at him uncertainly. 'No...?'

He gave her a smile. 'This may be out of character—out of my character to date,' he added knowingly. 'Old-fashioned, even. But, the truth is, Darci, I do not want to pre-empt our wedding night—*your* wedding night. You're everything to me, Darci. *Everything!* And I want everything to be perfect for you. Including our wedding,' he told her firmly as she would have protested. 'Although...' He frowned slightly as he released her, before moving determinedly to the edge of the bed to stand up.

Darci looked up at him, still slightly dazed by the intensity of her response to him. A response she was sure she would always have to this gorgeously sexy man she loved beyond reason, beyond doubt.

'Luc...?' she said, as he walked around the bed to stand beside her.

He smiled at her—a bright, dazzling, loving smile. 'Putting your happiness above everything else starts right now, Darci,' he promised her as he dropped down onto one knee and took one of her hands in his much larger ones. 'Will you marry me, Darci? Will you be my love for the rest of our lives? Will you be my wife, Darci?'

'Oh, yes, Luc. Yes, yes, *yes*!' she assured him tearfully.

'This time I do not in the least mind your answer being in triplicate!' he told her fiercely, and he moved to gather her up in his arms and kissed her until she was once again soft and wanton in his arms.

'As long as we don't *have* triplets,' Darci murmured ruefully. Although the thought of that, of having Luc's children, really wasn't in the least daunting.

'No doubt my mother would not complain—'

'Your *mother*, Luc!' Darci remembered, suddenly stricken. 'What on earth must she think of me after seeing us together like that earlier?'

'My mother is in absolutely no doubt as to what I think of you, my love,' Luc assured huskily. 'I told her before I came upstairs that I love you, and that if you would have me, I intended making you my wife,' he explained, at Darci's questioning look. 'I am sure that even now she is downstairs—probably with the rest of my family, too!—making wedding plans,' he said.

'You really told her that about me?' Darci breathed dazedly.

'Oh, yes,' he affirmed.

Darci swallowed hard. 'What did she say?'

He smiled. 'That I am her youngest beloved son.' His voice deepened with emotion. 'It's strange, Darci. As a child I only felt excluded from my parents' love—maybe because I am that youngest son. But tonight I have realised that my mother's love for me is unreserved—that she wants only my happiness.'

Darci's arms tightened about him. 'I'm glad, Luc. So very glad,' she told him shakily.

'In any case,' he continued briskly, 'my mother approves of you, and she is greatly looking forward to welcoming you into our family,' he announced with some of the arrogance Darci had noted tonight in all the Gambrelli men.

The Gambrelli men.

Cesare, Wolf and Luc.

And she was going to marry, to be the wife, the lifetime love, of the last—the very best!—of them….

Luc's arms tightened about her. 'When will you marry me, Darci?'

She glowed up at him. 'Well, as you've put this embargo on our lovemaking, perhaps it had better be soon, hmm? *Very* soon,' she added with feeling.

Luc gave a slow smile, a smile completely without reserve, and his eyes glowed with the deep love he felt for her. 'The fact that I would like your wedding night to be exactly that does not mean that we have to completely deny ourselves…' he pointed out.

'No?' Darci looked up at him with tempting green eyes.

'Most definitely no,' he assured her, as his lips trailed fire down the sensitive column of her throat, igniting desire.

'Oh, good…' she declared, before giving herself up to the wonder, the sheer delight, of being loved by Luc.

Her Gambrelli man.

* * * * *

Chapter 1

October
New York City

Nicole Masters was sitting cross-legged on her sofa while a cold autumn rain peppered the windows of her fourth-floor apartment. She was poking at the ice cream in her bowl and trying not to be in a mood.

Six weeks ago, a simple trip to her neighborhood pharmacy had turned into a nightmare. She'd walked into the middle of a robbery. She never even saw the man who shot her in the head and left her for dead. She'd survived, but some of her senses had not. She was dealing with short-term memory loss and a tendency to stagger. Even though she'd been told the problems were most likely temporary, she waged a daily battle with depression.

Her parents had been killed in a car wreck when she was twenty-one. And except for a few friends—and most recently her boyfriend, Dominic Tucci, who lived in the apartment right above hers, she was alone. Her doctor kept reminding her that she should be grateful to be alive, and on one level she knew he was right. But he wasn't living in her shoes.

If she'd been anywhere else but at that pharmacy when the robbery happened, she wouldn't have died twice on the way to the hospital. Instead of being grateful that she'd survived, she couldn't stop thinking of what she'd lost.

But that wasn't the end of her troubles. On top of everything else, something strange was happening inside her head. She'd begun to hear odd things: sounds, not voices—at least, she didn't think it was voices. It was more like the distant noise of rapids—a rush of wind and water inside her head that, when it came, blocked out everything around her. It didn't happen often, but when it did, it was frightening, and it was driving her crazy.

The blank moments, which is what she called them, even had a rhythm. First there came that sound, then a cold sweat, then panic with no reason. Part of her feared it was the beginning of an emotional breakdown. And part of her feared it wasn't—that it was going to turn out to be a permanent souvenir of her resurrection.

Frustrated with herself and the situation as it stood, she upped the sound on the TV remote. But instead of *Wheel of Fortune,* an announcer broke in with a special bulletin.

"This just in. Police are on the scene of a kidnapping that occurred only hours ago at The Dakota. Molly Dane, the six-year-old daughter of one of Hollywood's block-buster stars, Lyla Dane, was taken by force from the family apartment. At this time they have yet to receive a ransom demand. The housekeeper was seriously injured during the abduction, and is, at the present time, in surgery. Police are hoping to be able to talk to her once she regains consciousness. In the meantime, we are going now to a press conference with Lyla Dane."

Horrified, Nicole stilled as the cameras went live to where the actress was speaking before a bank of microphones. The shock and terror in Lyla Dane's voice were physically painful to watch. But even though Nicole kept upping the volume, the sound continued to fade.

Just when she was beginning to think something was wrong with her set, the broadcast suddenly switched from the Dane press conference to what appeared to be footage of the kidnapping, beginning with footage from inside the apartment.

When the front door suddenly flew back against the wall and four men rushed in, Nicole gasped. Horrified, she quickly realized that this must have been caught on a security camera inside the Dane apartment.

As Nicole continued to watch, a small Asian woman, who she guessed was the maid, rushed forward in an effort to keep them out. When one of the men hit her in the face with his gun, Nicole moaned. The violence was too reminiscent of what she'd lived through. Sick to her stomach, she fisted her hands against her belly, wishing it was over, but unable to tear her gaze away.

When the maid dropped to the carpet, the same man followed with a vicious kick to the little woman's midsection that lifted her off the floor.

"Oh, my God," Nicole said. When blood began to pool beneath the maid's head, she started to cry.

As the tape played on, the four men split up in different directions. The camera caught one running down a long marble hallway, then disappearing into a room. Moments later he reappeared, carrying a little girl, who Nicole assumed was Molly Dane. The child was wearing a pair of red pants and a white turtleneck sweater, and her hair was partially blocking her abductor's face as he carried her down the hall. She was kicking and screaming in his arms, and when he slapped her, it elicited an agonized scream that brought the other three running. Nicole watched in horror as one of them ran up and put his hand over Molly's face. Seconds later, she went limp.

One moment they were in the foyer, then they were gone.

Nicole jumped to her feet, then staggered drunkenly. The bowl of ice cream she'd absentmindedly placed in her lap shattered at her feet, splattering glass and melting ice cream everywhere.

The picture on the screen abruptly switched from the kidnapping to what Nicole assumed was a rerun of Lyla Dane's plea for her daughter's safe return, but she was numb.

Before she could think what to do next, the doorbell rang. Startled by the unexpected sound, she shakily swiped at the tears and took a step forward. She didn't feel the glass shards piercing her feet until she took the second step. At that point, sharp pains shot through her foot. She gasped, then looked down in confusion. Her legs looked as if she'd been running through mud, and she was standing in broken glass and ice cream, while a thin ribbon of blood seeped out from beneath her toes.

"Oh, no," Nicole mumbled, then stifled a second moan of pain.

The doorbell rang again. She shivered, then clutched her head in confusion.

"Just a minute!" she yelled, then tried to sidestep the rest of the debris as she hobbled to the door.

When she looked through the peephole in the door, she didn't know whether to be relieved or regretful.

It was Dominic, and as usual, she was a mess.

Nicole smiled a little self-consciously as she opened the

door to let him in. "I just don't know what's happening to me. I think I'm losing my mind."

"Hey, don't talk about my woman like that."

Nicole rode the surge of delight his words brought. "So I'm still your woman?"

Dominic lowered his head.

Their lips met.

The kiss proceeded.

Slowly.

Thoroughly.

* * * * *

Be sure to look for the AFTERSHOCK *anthology next month, as well as other exciting paranormal stories from Silhouette Nocturne.*
Available in October wherever books are sold.

REQUEST YOUR FREE BOOKS!

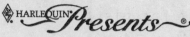 HARLEQUIN *Presents* ®

2 FREE NOVELS PLUS 2 FREE GIFTS!

YES! Please send me 2 FREE Harlequin Presents® novels and my 2 FREE gifts (gifts are worth about $10). After receiving them, if I don't wish to receive any more books, I can return the shipping statement marked "cancel". If I don't cancel, I will receive 6 brand-new novels every month and be billed just $4.05 per book in the U.S. or $4.74 per book in Canada, plus 25¢ shipping and handling per book and applicable taxes, if any*. That's a savings of close to 15% off the cover price! I understand that accepting the 2 free books and gifts places me under no obligation to buy anything. I can always return a shipment and cancel at any time. Even if I never buy another book, the two free books and gifts are mine to keep forever.

106 HDN ERRW 306 HDN ERRL

Name	(PLEASE PRINT)
Address	Apt. #
City	State/Prov.	Zip/Postal Code

Signature (if under 18, a parent or guardian must sign)

Mail to the **Harlequin Reader Service:**
IN U.S.A.: P.O. Box 1867, Buffalo, NY 14240-1867
IN CANADA: P.O. Box 609, Fort Erie, Ontario L2A 5X3

Not valid to current subscribers of Harlequin Presents books.

Want to try two free books from another line?
Call 1-800-873-8635 or visit www.morefreebooks.com.

* Terms and prices subject to change without notice. N.Y. residents add applicable sales tax. Canadian residents will be charged applicable provincial taxes and GST. Offer not valid in Quebec. This offer is limited to one order per household. All orders subject to approval. Credit or debit balances in a customer's account(s) may be offset by any other outstanding balance owed by or to the customer. Please allow 4 to 6 weeks for delivery. Offer available while quantities last.

Your Privacy: Harlequin Books is committed to protecting your privacy. Our Privacy Policy is available online at www.eHarlequin.com or upon request from the Reader Service. From time to time we make our lists of customers available to reputable third parties who may have a product or service of interest to you. If you would prefer we not share your name and address, please check here. ☐

HP08R

HARLEQUIN *Presents*

Wedlocked!

Legally wed,
But he's
never said,
"I love you."
They're…
Wedlocked!

**The series where marriages are made in haste…
and love comes later….**

Chef Lara needs cash—fast. Tall, dark, brooding
Wolfe Alexander needs to marry, and sees his opportunity.
He'll help Lara if she'll be his convenient wife….

Available in October

PURCHASED:
HIS PERFECT WIFE
by Helen Bianchin
#2763

Look out for more WEDLOCKED! marriage stories
coming soon in Harlequin Presents.

MEDITERRANEAN DOCTORS

Demanding, devoted and
drop-dead gorgeous—
These Latin doctors will
make your heart race!

Smolderingly sexy Mediterranean doctors

Saving lives by day...red-hot lovers by night

**Read these four Mediterranean Doctors stories
in this new collection by your favorite authors,
available in Presents EXTRA October 2008:**